Knee Deep in the Game

Knee Deep in the Game

Boston George

www.urbanbooks.net

Urban Books, LLC
78 East Industry Court
Deer Park, NY 11729

ISBN 13: 978-1-60162-294-5
ISBN 10: 1-60162-294-5

First Printing November 2010
Printed in the United States of America

10 9 8 7 6 5 4 3 2 1

This is a work of fiction. Any references or similarities to actual events, real people, living, or dead, or to real locales are intended to give the novel a sense of reality. Any similarity in other names, characters, places, and incidents is entirely coincidental.

Distributed by Kensington Publishing Corp.
Submit Wholesale Orders to:
Kensington Publishing Corp.
C/O Penguin Group (USA) Inc.
Attention: Order Processing
405 Murray Hill Parkway
East Rutherford, NJ 07073-2316
Phone: 1-800-526-0275
Fax: 1-800-227-9604

Knee Deep in the Game

A Novel by Boston George

"How far are you willing to go for your come-up?"

Chapter One

"Damn, I'm hungrier than a mu'fucka," Pop said to himself as he heard his stomach growling out loud. He was hungry, but his appetite was for cash and at that point he would do anything to get it. *What the fuck is taking this fool so long?* he wondered as he stood anxiously in front of his building. Pop waited, his patience growing thin as each minute passed by. A smile spread across his face when he saw the Chinese-food delivery woman riding around the corner on her bike with a bag of food hanging from the handlebars. *'Bout fuckin' time,* he thought. Pop quickly ran into the lobby and waited for the Chinese woman to come in the building. Standing by the mailboxes, Pop noticed it was a lobby full of people waiting for the elevator to come.

"Fuck that, I'm making my move anyway," Pop whispered as he hit the button buzzing the Chinese woman into the building.

"Yo, how much is it?" he asked casually as he went into his pocket to appear as if he were reaching for money.

Before the Chinese woman could respond Pop punched her in the face. The blow sent her stumbling back into the door, causing a loud noise to erupt throughout the building. Desperate to get out of Dodge, Pop hurriedly tried grabbing the bag out of the Chinese woman's hands but her grip was too strong.

***

Pop instantly caught the woman with a powerful right hook to the stomach. When he saw the woman doubled over, clutching her stomach, he quickly followed up with a left uppercut, knocking the Chinese lady out cold.

"Hey, what are you doing to that lady?" a woman who was waiting for the elevator screamed.

Pop ignored her and viciously dug in the Chinese lady's pockets like a vulture until he found a handful of crumpled-up bills. He quickly stuffed the money in his pocket, grabbed the bagful of Chinese food, and fled into the staircase.

"I can't stand that dirty boy, that's why Chinese people don't like to deliver to the projects no more," one of the bystanders commented as they looked down at the bloody Chinese lady who was laid out in the middle of the lobby floor. "You know that's the fifth time this week he's done this!" another nosy lady stated once Pop was out of earshot. She didn't dare speak up in the middle of the act, in fear of seeing the wrath of the young, wild thug.

"You lying!" another person stated in shock, encouraging the woman to keep talking so that she could get filled in on the hood gossip.

Pop went straight to the roof and enjoyed his Chinese food in peace, because he knew if he had gone home, he would not have been able to enjoy his food with all of the people who lived in his house.

Pop hated that he had to steal every night just to eat, but what other choice did he have? He wasn't as heartless as it seemed, he was just a li'l nigga out for self. He had no other choice but to get his meals how he could. He didn't grow up in a fairy tale where hot dinner and early breakfast was served by Mother and Father. He was from the projects and his mother had lost her soul there before he could even remember. His mother was a crackhead/prostitute, with five children who she did very little for. So some people might think he was running around terrorizing innocent people, but Pop was simply trying to survive . . . the best way he could. Pop hated his life and he didn't give a fuck about anyone but himself. He looked at it like people were on this earth just to die, so why give a fuck? Do what you can and get as much as you can before you leave this muthafucka . . . straight up.

After his meal Pop decided to go home and get some rest. As soon as he stepped foot in the apartment he could tell just by looking at his mother that she was high as a kite. She had a smoker's gaze in her eyes. It was an expression that he had become accustomed to. He couldn't remember the last time that his mother had looked him in the eyes without the affects of a crack high clouding her vision.

"Where the fuck you been all mu'fuckin' day?" Teresa snarled, looking her second oldest son up and down.

"Out," Pop shot back as he stepped over piles of clothes and garbage that laid all over the floor.

"Don't walk away from me while I'm talking to you, you son of a bitch, you don't have no manners," Teresa fussed in an icy tone as she grabbed Pop's arm.

"Yeah, I wonder why," Pop responded disrespectfully as he jerked his arm loose.

Teresa was about to hit him upside the head with a broom, until she heard somebody knocking on the door. She was expecting one of her regular customers and quickly forgot all about her son. She rushed to the bathroom and tried to fix herself up in the mirror. What had once been a pretty girl was now a worn-out woman who had been swallowed whole by the streets, but pussy was pussy and men were willing to pay for it as long as she serviced them correctly.

When Teresa opened the front door, the ugliest mu'fucka in the world stood on the other side.

"Hey, John. What's up, baby?" Teresa greeted with a fake smile on her face.

You tell me, sexy," John replied. Strong, hard liquor lingered on his breath as if he himself knew that he needed to be drunk in order to enjoy the sex he had with Teresa.

"Why don't you come in my room so we can talk in private," She suggested as the two went inside the bedroom.

Pop lay down on the floor in his room that he shared with his three brothers and one sister, trying to sleep. The constant knocking of his mother's headboard against the wall and her screams of passion made it hard for him to sleep. He couldn't ignore the disgusting sounds of her sexing her client. The thought of it turned his stomach.

"Fuck this shit," Pop said to himself as he threw on his rundown sneakers and headed back outside.

Pop hated being in his mother's house. Some nights he would even break day outside on the bench, just so he wouldn't have to deal with the woman who had given him birth. Teresa treated Pop the worst, mainly because he looked so much like his father, who she hated. To have Pop sitting in her face all day reminding her of the man who had broken her heart was too much for Teresa to bear, so she took her frustrations out on him, blaming him for her life's misfortunes and destroying their relationship beyond repair.

When Pop made it outside he sat on the bench just chilling, eating some Doritos with the money he stole from the Chinese delivery woman. As he sat on the bench, he noticed the sexiest Spanish chick he had ever seen before walk past.

"Damn, shorty is banging," Pop mumbled as his eyes followed her behind as she switched from side to side in her tight-fitting, spandex jeans. The sway of her hips hypnotized him as he noticed the gap between her thighs. "One of these days I'm going to bag shorty," Pop said to himself as he watched the woman disappear inside the building. Even though the Spanish diva paid him no mind, Pop was determined to get her attention some way, somehow. He always noticed the girl coming in and out of the projects, but she never spoke to anybody; everytime he saw her she was on the move. Pop didn't know, when, where, or how, but he knew he was going to make her his girl. His thoughts were interrupted when his friend, Mike, came walking up.

"What's goodie?" Mike asked, giving Pop a pound.

"Ain't shit, I'm just out here chilling," Pop replied, his thoughts still focused on his dream girl.

Mike wasn't really a good friend, just somebody Pop used to play ball with or smoke a blunt with every now and then. Mike was a good kid whose main focus was on school. Pop, on the other hand, hated school and made sure he cut class every chance he got so the two were cool, but it wasn't nothing serious.

"Why you sitting over here looking all lonely, nigga? Let's go to the courts and shoot some hoops," Mike suggested.

"You talking like you want to play for some money?" Pop challenged.

"You not tired of me taking your money yet?" Mike countered, his testosterone rising.

"Don't talk me to death. We gonna do this or what?" Pop asked, cutting to the chase.

"You ain't said nothing but a word," Mike responded as the two got up and headed to the park.

***

"Yo, Rusty, did them two niggas you sent to pick up that money for me ever come back?" Fresh asked, taking a long drag from his finger-thick blunt.

"Nah, them clowns got locked up; those stupid mu'fuckas went to go rob somebody before the pickup and got caught," Rusty answered while shaking his head in disgrace.

"Damn, those were our last two soldiers," Fresh barked, not believing how stupid these young kids were now days. "Fuck is wrong with these stupid mu'fuckas, man. I was teaching 'em how to get money . . . all they had to do was lay in the cut and let the paper come to them but they want to try their hands at the stickup game."

"I know, I guess we're going to have to find us some new goons," Rusty answered as he took the blunt. "Don't worry, we'll have a whole new goon squad within the next two days. It shouldn't be hard to find some local wannabe tough guys dying to prove how hard they are," Rusty assured his partner.

"Nah B,. I'm not fuckin' wit' no more clowns, we been getting real sloppy since Tito got locked up. I'm starting off fresh this time just like my name, you dig? I'm recruiting all the new soldiers myself," Fresh said, in deep thought.

"That's cool. I'll hold things down until you find us a new goon squad, plus Tito will be home next year," Rusty reminded him.

Tito was Fresh's number-one soldier who had been riding with him since day one. Tito was nothing more than a troublemaker with nothing going for himself until Fresh recruited the young man straight off the streets. Fresh trained the young beast from scratch, molding him into one of the most feared cats on the streets. Once Tito made himself a large amount of money there was no stopping him. Tito was what you call a go-to type of nigga.

If somebody needed to be shot, Tito was the man.

If there was money to be picked up, Tito was the man.

If somebody needed to be hung out of a window or thrown off the roof, Tito was the man for that too.

He was a twenty-four-year-old Spanish kid who loved his job a little too much. He loved being an enforcer . . . the only problem was he got caught up trying to help a family member get out of a jam. He held a gun to the head of some middle-school kid who had been harassing his little sister, and wound up going to jail and getting sentenced to two years. He already served one year and now had one year left to go.

"Yo, I'm about to go pick up my shorty real quick. I'm going to need you to do me a favor. I need you to go to the Bronx for me and pick up that paper that Randy got for me," Fresh ordered as he gave Rusty a pound and headed out the door.

Fresh walked over to the curb with his hand discreetly placed over his pistol just in case there were niggas lurking, waiting to knock him off his throne. He made sure he looked over both shoulders before he hopped in his gray Range Rover and pulled off. Fresh was a major player in the street game and couldn't afford no fuckups, plus his pops—who used to be a major player back in the day—had schooled him on the game. One thing his father always told him was, "Never do something that will jeopardize what you love the most." So with that advice in the back of his mind, Fresh never really got his hands too dirty unless he had to. Instead, he hired a goon squad to take care of everything that might jeopardize his freedom and his money. Don't get it twisted, however; Fresh was no chump. In order to get to the top he had to do what he had to do. At a young age he had wars with the best of the best, and was still standing strong . . . the results were, at the age of twenty-eight, he was already a street legend and proud of it.

When Fresh pulled up in front of the projects he hopped out and paid a young kid fifty dollars to watch his truck. The kid could not have been any older than ten and when he saw the huge face on the bill his eyes bulged in excitement.

"Keep that for yourself, shorty," Fresh said as he gave the young gangster a pound and kept it moving.

Everybody looked and treated Fresh like he was a movie star or some kind of celebrity. Every girl in the projects wanted to fuck him. His hood status was top-notch and chicks lied constantly just to make it seem like they had dealt with him before. Everybody knew that if you fucked with Fresh then you were instantly upgraded, because Fresh never chose a bum bitch. He was highly selective and only the crème de la crème were fortunate enough to share his time or his bed. A gold-digging bitch need not apply because Fresh only dealt with dimes and could see straight through a hood rat. He had a certain arrogance about himself that women found irresistible and that niggas around the way attempted to mimic. He was a boss and as he walked past the onlookers he gave them a nod and a smile . . . surely making their day.

When Fresh stepped in the pissy elevator, his nose immediately wrinkled from the odor that viciously assaulted his nose. He did his best to ignore the smell as he pressed his call button for his floor. The elevator was so filthy he thought that even the bottom of his sneaks were too clean for the trifling space. He held his breath as the elevator sprang into motion. When he reached his floor he quickly headed down the skinny hallway until he found the door he was looking for. After a light knock, Amanda, his shorty, came to the door wearing nothing but a silk robe.

"Hey, *papi, que pasa?*" The Dominican woman greeted, saying "what's up?" She was happy to see him and the husky tone of her strong accent let him know that she had been waiting and had something good in store for him.

"My fault I'm late, but I had to take care of something," Fresh answered as he stepped inside the nicely furnished apartment.

As Fresh headed to the back room with Amanda, he saw her younger sister sitting in the living room.

"What's good, Melissa?" Fresh asked as he playfully closed the book she was reading.

"Hey, Fresh, nothing; just studying," Melissa answered.

"A'ight, you make sure you keep them grades up, you dig? A mind is a terrible thing to waste," Fresh stated as he quickly disappeared into the bedroom with Amanda.

Amanda and Melissa lived alone in a two-bedroom apartment. Fresh paid all the bills in the apartment because the two sisters were in school and had no income coming in. Fresh and Amanda had been dating for three and a half years. A year into the relationship Amanda's mother died from a heart attack. So instead of the two sisters getting put out on the streets, Fresh decided to take care of all the bills so the two sisters wouldn't have to drop out of school and worry about doing odd jobs to pay the rent. He couldn't let this girl be put out in the streets, so he made sure she was comfortable and gave her most of the things she asked for.

"How long I got you for this time?" Amanda asked in a snotty tone.

"Not long, I have to go downtown and check up on a few things in a hot minute," he told her.

"*Papi*, why you always do this to me?" Amanda asked, pouting like a baby.

"Baby, I have to get this money. I'm going to be busy this

whole week, but I promise next week will be our week, all right?" He kissed her.

"You promise?" Amanda asked as she slid Into Fresh's lap.

"You know I got you," Fresh replied, looking into her hazel eyes.

"*Viene aqui, papi,*" Amanda whispered, instructing him to come over to her as she stood up and dropped her robe. Under her robe, she stood wearing nothing but a rainbow-colored thong.

It was something about Dominican woman he just couldn't resist. Their light skin, long, naturally curly hair, and voluptuous but tight physiques intrigued him and as he stared at Amanda his dick instantly grew hard. He immediately fondled one of her nice-sized, firm breasts in his mouth, her nipple growing long and hard as he sucked on it like he was waiting for milk to come out.

"Oh, *papi,*" Amanda moaned as she ran her nails down Fresh's back.

Once Amanda's pussy was soaking wet, she turned into an animal, aggressively unbuckling Fresh's belt until she found what she was looking for.

Amanda threw her long, curly hair in a ponytail, then placed Fresh's already hard dick in her mouth and went to work. She licked and slobbered all over her man's love tool, making all kinds of sexy noises with her mouth and working her hands up and down the shaft with just enough pressure to make his toes curl. When Amanda finished giving her man a nice spit shine, she hopped into the bed on all fours. "Come on, papi, hurt me," she whined, looking like a porno star.

Fresh did as he was told, and got right to work.

"*Ooh, mas papi, mas, mas,*" Amanda screamed, loving every stroke as she begged him for more and more. With each stroke Fresh went deeper and deeper. He gripped both of her ass cheeks and spread them apart as he plunged in and out of her love tunnel.

Fresh piped his girl down until he couldn't take it anymore. As soon as he was about to explode, he quickly pulled out and came all over Amanda's fat, but firm butt cheeks. Before he could even finish putting his clothes on, he noticed that Amanda was already falling asleep.

"My work here is done," Fresh said, chuckling, as he headed out the door.

Chapter Two

"Boy, get your lazy ass up!" Teresa yelled, poking Pop in the ribs with a broomstick.

"What you want?" Pop growled, wiping the crust from his eyes.

"I want you to get a job and go to school, but we know that's not happening," she said, rolling her eyes. "Go to the store and get me a loaf of bread." Teresa tossed Pop three quarters and began to walk out of the room.

"Yo, dis not even enough," Pop called back angrily.

"Make it enough," Teresa shot back, snaking her neck.

"I can't wait 'til I get some money so I can get the fuck up out of here," Pop huffed as he stormed past his mother.

"I can't wait either, mu'fucka!" Teresa yelled over her shoulder before Pop walked out the door.

"A yo, ock' I'm going to need some bread, but I only got seventy-five cents. I'll pay you back when my moms get her welfare check," Pop said, feeling embarrassed that he was short again.

"It's okay, B. I know how it be sometimes," the Arab responded, trying extra hard to sound cool.

As Pop exited the store and headed toward his building, he saw an old lady coming in his direction. He noticed she was wearing way too much jewelry for a woman of her age. *Fuck, she walking around here jeweled from head to toe? I should take that shit just because she's asking for it,* he thought as he eyed the woman.

"Nah, I'm not robbing no old lady," Pop said, trying to talk himself out of doing something stupid, but he just couldn't resist. His main objective was to save up enough money so he could move out of his mother's house, and that old lady was the perfect come-up.

When Pop got close enough to the old lady he quickly snatched her necklace, followed by her pocketbook. Once he had what he wanted, he violently pushed the old lady to the ground as he took off running into his building. When he made it upstairs he made sure he caught his breath before entering his house to avoid any unnecessary questioning from his mother.

"What the fuck took you so long?" Teresa barked.

"The store was crowded," he lied.

"Yeah right, you lying bastard, that's why I hate sending you to the store," Teresa snarled as she snatched the loaf of bread from his hands.

"If I take so long, then go to the store yourself next time," Pop said with ice in his tone, as he walked back out the door.

"You better watch your nasty-ass mouth, boy, before you get your ass whipped in this mu'fucka!" Teresa yelled, hoping Pop heard her.

Pop headed straight to the staircase, where he left the old lady's pocketbook.

"Jackpot," he said, finding $400 cash in the pocketbook.

"Fuck that, I need this more than her," he reasoned as he tossed the pocketbook on the staircase floor and headed outside.

When he stepped outside, he saw a big crowd in front of the next building.

"What the fuck is going on over there?" Pop wondered, looking at the sea of black faces.

When he got closer, he saw that it was just Fresh and his crew that drew all the attention.

"Fuck them niggas," Pop said to himself as he sat over on an empty bench. He didn't know Fresh, but he knew who he was and what he was about, and so did everybody else who lived in the projects.

Pop sat on the bench, watching Fresh's crew sell drugs like it was water. "Them fools don't even know what to do with all that money," Pop commented bitterly as he imagined himself being in their shoes.

Ten minutes later he noticed some diesel guy walking toward him. Pop, not being a fool, could smell beef from a mile away. He knew that there was bad blood just from the screw face that the dude was giving him. Pop quickly hopped up off the bench to stand his ground.

"Hey, my man, is your name Pop?" the big guy asked, cracking his knuckles.

"Maybe," Pop answered nonchalantly as he pulled up his sagging pants and stared the dude directly in his eyes. Despite the fact that the guy was twice his size, he was determined to let him know that there was not a bitch bone in his body.

"Yo, I don't got time for games. Either you Pop or you not! That mu'fucka robbed my grandmother. You better hope you not him!" the big man yelled, talking with his hands and making a scene. Pop had learned early on that a loud nigga was a scared nigga. If someone really was about their business then all the talking wasn't necessary.

"So you wanna fight over an old wrinkled bitch?" Pop said as he threw a quick jab, catching the big man in his mouth.

"That's all you got?" the big man asked, not even being

fazed by the jab. In one quick motion the big man threw a wild haymaker, trying to take Pop's head off.

Pop quickly sidestepped the haymaker, and caught him with a short left hook followed by a right uppercut.

"Yo, them niggas over there getting 'em on," Fresh said as he and the whole crowd headed over to see the fight.

The big man knew his hand skills were no match for the young kid, so he went to plan B. He grabbed Pop in a bear hug, and then belly to belly slammed him on the hard concrete. The impact of his back against the concrete knocked the wind out of Pop and he grimaced in pain as the whole crowd erupted in oohs and aahs when they saw Pop get slammed to the ground. "Goddamn," some kid in a white T-shirt said, looking on in amazement.

Once the big man was on top of Pop, he started throwing punches from every angle. Pop did everything he could to get the big man off him, but nothing he did seemed to work, so he just balled up in a fetal position, trying to block as many punches as he could.

When Fresh saw the fight getting out of hand, he quickly stepped in and broke it up.

"Yo, that's enough. Get off the li'l nigga," Fresh said, pushing the big man off of Pop.

"Don't put your mu'fuckin' hands on—" The big man held on to the rest of his sentence when he realized who had pushed him.

"Get the fuck up out of here," Fresh nonchalantly said, dismissing the big man. Without saying a word the big man walked off a winner, but felt like a loser inside.

"Yo, shorty, you okay?" Fresh asked, helping Pop get back to his feet.

"Yeah, I'm good, I had that clown right where I wanted

him," Pop responded as he dusted himself off and headed toward his building. Fresh stood silent as he watched the young soldier walk away with his head held high.

"Little mu'fucka got heart," Fresh said to himself as he watched Pop walk away. "Yo, Rusty, who is that li'l nigga?"

"Some li'l street punk, he's a real scumbag, loser-type nigga," Rusty answered, laughing.

"I like that li'l nigga's style," Fresh said to himself as he hopped in his Range Rover and peeled off.

Amanda sat on the 1 train watching two bums sing and dance for spare change.

"Some people will do anything for a high," she said to herself as she finished watching the bums perform. Amanda hated riding the train in New York; there were just too many people in the city. She was going to take her road test in a week, because Fresh wouldn't let her drive without a license and when she did, she wouldn't be caught dead on another train. She used to always get Fresh to drive her places, but after a while he put an end to that. He was a busy man and didn't have time to be driving her all over the place, so he told her if she was tired of taking the train, then she better learn how to drive.

When Amanda finally made it home she stripped naked and hopped in the shower. She aimed the shower head directly on her face and let the warm water massage her scalp as she washed her sins away. After her shower she laid spread across her king-sized bed, naked. Her fingers began to take on a mind of their own as she fondled her nipple with one hand and rubbed her clitoris in circles with the other. Feeling her sex rise and the sticky wetness on her fingertips, she tasted herself, putting one sweet finger in her mouth. She was horny and needed her man.

I wonder what Fresh is doing? she thought to herself as she picked up the phone and dialed his number.

"I thought you forgot about me for a minute," Vanessa said as she answered the door naked. As Fresh stared lustfully at Vanessa's voluptuous figure, he licked his lips in anticipation. She was so different from Amanda. Her five feet five inch frame, wide hips, and firm behind were the complete opposite of Amanda, but he was feeling her all the same. He was a hustler who could have any chick he wanted on his arm. He knew it was wrong, but it was all in the game. Although he loved his girl, one woman wasn't enough. New pussy always excited him, which is why his dick rocked instantly at the sight of Vanessa's flawless body. He adjusted his hardness in his jeans as he stepped into her apartment.

"You know I was coming to see you, I just had to take care of something real quick," Fresh responded, looking at Vanessa's body glowing from all the baby oil she covered her body with.

"Come give me some love, I haven't seen you in two weeks," Vanessa said as she jumped up on Fresh, wrapping her legs around his waist.

"I missed you baby," she whispered as she gave Fresh a wet, sloppy kiss.

"I missed you, too" Fresh replied, roughly tossing Vanessa on the bed.

"Bring that dick over here," Vanessa said once all of his clothes were removed.

Vanessa aggressively slammed him on the satin sheets that

laid on her queen-sized bed. She straddled her legs on Fresh and winced as he spread her love wide open with his thickness. Vanessa bounced until he filled her, then contracted her muscles as she lifted her knees and slid up and down his pole. Fresh lifted his head to watch his member disappear into her flesh and he rotated his hips in an attempt to match her stroke. Vanessa abruptly stopped and kissed his lips before swallowing his dick down her deep throat. She licked him from the tip of his manhood to the entrance of his backside, while she stroked him and fondled his balls.

"Oh, shit," he moaned as he put his hands in her hair and guided her up and down, making her appear as if she were bobbing for apples. She hopped back on top and rode him backward, giving him a magnificent view of her voluptuous ass cheeks. He parted them, wet his finger, and tickled her crack.

"Boy, you know that makes me cum," she whined. "Stop, Fresh . . . I want to ride this dick all day."

Her pleas fell on deaf ears, because Fresh continued to stroke her crack until he reached her anus. He stuck a finger inside and she sucked him in like a vacuum. She began to ride him faster, her big behind bouncing on his balls, causing shivers to run the length of his spine. She worked her muscles and clapped her ass cheeks all while he fingered her hole until they both climaxed in ecstasy. The ringing of his cell phone interrupted them. Fresh tapped her on the behind gently, signaling for her to get up so that he could retrieve the call. He reached for his pants and looked at the caller ID to see that it was Amanda. He put his finger to his lips to signal for Vanessa to be quiet. She rolled her eyes, knowing that it had to be another bitch and got up from the bed as Fresh took his call. She wanted to tell him not to disrespect her by talking to his chick right in front of her, but she knew her place. She was happy to just have her spot in his life. A lot of women around her way would kill to be Fresh's side chick, so she had to play her position. She'd rather be number two than have no spot on the team at all.

"Hey, baby, what's good?" he answered.

"Nothing. I was thinking about you. What you doing?"

"Chilling down town with this nigga, Rusty," Fresh lied.

"Okay, baby, handle your business. When you finish, come by and check me, if it's not too late," she said, her woman's intuition kicking in, making her feel insecure.

"I got you, baby," Fresh replied, flipping his phone closed. He looked toward Vanessa, who wore her heart on her sleeve. Her quivering lip, folded arms, and sad eyes were a clear indication that she was unhappy.

"How long am I going to be a secret?" Vanessa snarled, snaking her neck.

"Come on, don't start that shit," Fresh warned, brushing past her as he headed to the bathroom to clean up.

"Fuck that shit," Vanessa sighed. "I ain't nobody's secret, mu'fucka. I don't know why you always fuckin' with them Dominican bitches, anyway," Vanessa screamed loud enough so Fresh could hear her.

Fresh sighed and smartly replied, "Because Dominican bitches don't get at me with all that lip."

Vanessa stuck up her middle finger and he shook his head.

"Yo, listen this ain't no Dominican and black thing, I fuck wit' who I'm feeling, you dig? I don't want to hear that bullshit come out your mouth again," he stated firmly.

"I'm sorry, baby, I just want to be your main chick, you can't be mad at that," Vanessa said as tears flowed freely down her face.

"Vanessa, I don't have one main chick. Every chick plays a certain part in my life, smell me?" Fresh said, wiping away her tears.

"Yeah, I understand," Vanessa slurred.

Deep down inside Vanessa really loved Fresh, but she knew she would never be Fresh's number-one chick. She knew that she was playing herself by allowing him to have her and any other woman he wanted as well, but it was all in the game. She knew that he would never love her the way that she did him, so she took the little pieces of himself that he was willing to share. The lonely nights and broken promises were not enough to make her let him go. Fresh had gotten inside her head, which is why she put up with his shit. As Fresh put his clothes back on, she wished that he could stay, but she decided not to even make herself look stupid by asking.

"Okay, baby, be careful out there," Vanessa said, kissing Fresh on his lips as she watched him walk out the door.

When he stepped foot out of Vanessa's building he was met by Rusty and Pooh Bear.

Pooh Bear was a nineteen-year-old fat kid who would do anything if the price was right. He had been working for Fresh for a year and a half; he and Rusty were the only two loyal enforcers Fresh had left; everybody else were just workers and runners.

"Pooh, what's popping?" Fresh asked, giving the young man dap.

"Out here chasing the dollar as usual," Pooh replied.

"Yo, I'm going to need you to go to Queens and pick up that package Bamboo got waiting for me," Fresh instructed.

"Say no more," Pooh said as he walked to the corner to wave down a cab.

"Yo, I'm going to need you to do me a favor too," Fresh said, looking at Rusty.

"I need you to go to 142nd and Broadway and see why Papi and the rest of them Spanish mu'fuckas are taking so long to come up with that paper. After you talk to them clowns hit me up and let me know what's good."

"It's already done, my nigga," Rusty responded as the two men went their separate ways.

Chapter Three

"Damn, I have to hurry up and find me a vic," Pop said to himself as he noticed the sun starting to go down. Once again, Pop was starving. He hadn't eaten anything all day, but to him this was a daily routine. It was the same struggles a different day.

As Pop sat on the bench thinking about his next move, he saw his dream girl walk past, looking sexy as usual. Her long brown hair hung down to her butt, with her bang barely touching her eyebrows, and to top it off her ass was so big it looked like two asses in one.

"That's my word, that girl is going to be my future wife," Pop said to himself as he studied the Dominican girl as she walked through the projects to get to her building.

Pop's whole facial expression changed when he saw his dream girl stop and start talking to Fresh.

"Damn, that nigga got all the hoes," Pop said, admiring the young street legend.

"What you doing getting in this late?" Fresh asked as he stopped Melissa in front of the building.

"Nothing, I stayed after school for some extra credit," Melissa answered. "I'm surprised you're not upstairs with my sister," she said, letting out a light chuckle.

"Nah, I'm about to head downtown in a minute, but tell Amanda I'm going to call her later on tonight."

"Okay, I'll tell her. Be careful," Melissa said as she headed into the building.

As soon as Pop was about to give up and go home, a miracle happened.

"Excuse me, do you know which building is 3758?" a middle-aged white man asked.

"Yeah, it's right there," Pop said, pointing toward a building.

When the white guy looked to see which building the helpful young man was pointing to, Pop had already knocked him out with a sharp right hook to the temple.

He quickly searched through the white man's pockets, until he found the man's wallet.

"Good-looking fam," Pop chuckled, stepping over the white man's unconscious body.

When Fresh saw what happened a big smile appeared across his face. *That li'l nigga gives no fucks. He ruthless.*

"Hey, yo, shorty!" Fresh yelled.

"What's poppin'?" Pop asked defensively.

"Nice work back there," Fresh said as handed the young warrior $500 dollars.

"I'm looking for a good soldier like you. I been seeing you put in a lot of work around here lately," he told Pop.

"I'm just trying to eat, man. I got to do me," Pop said honestly.

"What's your name, shorty?"

"Pop," he answered.

"Everybody calls me Fresh. How 'bout you come take a ride with me?" Fresh posed it as a question, but it was more like a demand as he stepped away from the building, knowing that Pop would follow.

"A'ight bet," Pop replied.

With no hesitation he hopped in the passenger seat of the Range Rover.

Damn, this shits look like a fuckin' airplane, Pop thought as he looked at all the buttons and lights.

"I appreciate what you doing for me," Pop said, thankful for the $500 dollars he just received.

"Don't worry about it, shorty," Fresh said as he made the engine come to life and stepped on the gas.

Pop's eyes lit up when he saw Fresh pull up into the IHOP parking lot.

"You hungry, little homie?" Fresh asked, already knowing the answer.

"A little bit," Pop lied, trying to save face but deep down inside he was starving and literally would eat a horse.

The slim waitress escorted the two men to a booth in the back of the diner.

"How would you like to work for me?" Fresh asked, sipping on his water and getting straight to the chase.

"Work for you how? What would I have to do?" Pop questioned defensively.

"Listen, B. I know about your situation, and I'm just here to help," Fresh told him.

"How you going to help?"

"I'm going to help by putting some money in your fuckin' pocket," Fresh answered quickly.

"Why me? I'm pretty sure you got hundreds of people to choose from, people who would love to prove something to you."

"Because I see something in you that you don't even see in yourself," Fresh responded.

"And what's that?" Pop asked curiously.

"That's my little secret," Fresh laughed as the slim waitress brought them their food.

"So what does this job consist of?" Pop asked as he cut off a piece of his waffle and gobbled it up.

"I need you to be an enforcer for me," Fresh said bluntly to see where Pop's head was at. He had seen Pop go for broke so he knew that he had the heart.

"You mean a goonie," Pop corrected him.

"If that's what you want to call it. You won't be doing shit you haven't been doing already. You might have to beat a few people up, stab a few cats, hang 'em out the window—you know, regular shit," Fresh said nonchalantly, shrugging his shoulders. "Can you handle that?"

"Of course I can," Pop answered, happy to finally be on the winning team.

"If I'm going to be a goon, believe I'm going to be the best goon that ever lived," he said, accepting Fresh's proposition.

"This is the beginning to a great friendship," Fresh said as the two men's glasses clinked together. "If you be loyal to me, I will always be loyal to you," he said as he slowly sipped from his glass. "I love your heart."

"I'm just doing what I gotta do, it's never personal," Pop stated honestly.

"You ever heard of a guy named Bamboo?"

"I've heard the name but I don't know him, he could walk past me right now and I wouldn't even know that was him," Pop answered.

"Well, real soon I'm going to be shutting that cocksucker down, but I know it's not going to be easy. That's why if you down you gon' have to be down for whatever, you dig?" Fresh said, trying to read Pop's facial expression.

"I can dig it," Pop replied. "I take it you two don't get along."

"Well, as of right now he's the connect." Fresh began. "But he's a grimy-ass old nigga. Plus he not playing the game how it's supposed to be played, and we can't have that and since nobody else wants to take care of this problem, I figured why not step up to the plate," Fresh said with a smile.

"Fuck it," Pop said. "I don't see why not."

"They say if you want shit done the right way, then you gotta do it yourself," Fresh said nonchalantly.

Fresh sat back quietly and watched Pop attack his food. From the looks of things he could tell that the young man had not eaten anything all day, maybe even two. He had no remorse about putting Pop on his team. He was already a product of the hood. At least now he would be getting paid.

Before Pop went upstairs, he went to the Chinese restaurant to get his brothers and sister something to eat since he had a pocketful of money.

"Yo, bitch, hurry the fuck up with my order," some ghetto chick with blond streaks in her nicely-done weave yelled at the Chinese lady behind the counter. Pop chuckled to himself. It was just another day in the life for him. He lived in a jungle where even the females were cold and callous, but now he looked at his environment in an entirely new perspective. Working for Fresh was about to change his life. He wouldn't be down for long.

"Yo, let me get three orders of chicken wings and pork-fried rice," Pop ordered as he took a seat at the small table.

Pop couldn't believe the opportunity Fresh was giving him—not only did he get to beat people up, but he was now going to get paid for it. Things could not have been better for him.

"Yo ,bitch, you need to hurry up, I don't got all mu'fuckin' day, I have to be going in a minute," blond hair barked.

This bitch is wilding out, Pop said to himself as he continued to watch the show the ghetto woman put on.

"What the fuck is taking so long?" blonde asked, walking up to the counter.

"Your order will be ready in one minute," the Chinese lady said, trying to calm the ghetto woman down.

"Bitch, you said that shit twenty minutes ago—stop playing with me!" blonde hair said, ready to spaz out.

"Yo, ma, chill out before them Chinese mu'fuckas spit in your shit," Pop said, trying to defuse the situation.

"Spit in who shit?" blond hair asked, snaking her neck. "Please, I'll slap everybody back there," she said, pointing behind the counter.

"Here you go, ma'am" the Chinese lady said in a frail voice.

"It's about mu'fuckin' time," blond hair snarled as she snatched the bag out of the hands of the Chinese lady.

"I can't stand you mu'fuckas. Give me some more duck sauce too," she barked.

"Be cool shorty, and don't hurt nobody," Pop said, looking at the nice sized-ass on the ghetto light-skinned girl.

"I'ma try not to," she shot back with a smile as she walked out the Chinese restaurant.

"I might have to get up on that," Pop said, imagining him and Blondie going at it in a hotel room as he watched her walk off, switching her ass from side to side.

"Sir, your order is ready," the Chinese lady said, snapping him out of his daydream.

When Pop got home his brothers and sister were happy that he brought them something to eat.

"What the fuck is going on out here?" Teresa said, walking in the living room. "Where the fuck did you get money from?"

"Don't worry about it, just eat," Pop said sourly as he plopped down on the couch.

"Boy, when I ask you a straight question, you better give me a straight mu'fuckin' answer," Teresa shot back, standing in front of the TV, intentionally trying to make him mad.

"I found twenty dollars outside lying on the ground, so I picked it up and brought us some Chinese food," he said in an uninterested tone.

"You don't got no change?" Teresa asked, rolling her eyes.

"No, I don't got no change, and why does the whole house smell like shit?" Pop asked.

"Because the garbage is right there waiting for you to take it to the incinerator."

Instead of arguing, Pop emptied the garbage, went to his room, and went to sleep. Sleep was one way he always escaped from the shit hole he was living in. He would always have the same dream every night: He would always dream he was out of his mother's house, only to wake up to be disappointed and to face another fucked-up day.

The next morning Pop woke up to the sound of somebody beating up his mother. He quickly got up to investigate, but when he reached his mother's room her door was locked.

"Oh, well," he said coldheartedly as he got dressed and headed outside. He knew better than to get involved in his mother's drama. The last time he got involved, he ended up with a black eye and a swollen lip, all because Teresa stole some goods from one of her customers. This time Teresa would just have to hold it down by herself.

Pop ignored all the screams and cries for help as he exited the apartment without a care in the world.

When Pop made it outside, he saw Rusty waving him over.

"Youngin', you on the payroll now, yeah?" Rusty asked, revealing a mouthful of gold teeth.

"Yeah, Fresh put me on last night, he told me to report to you," Pop answered.

"A'ight, good, 'cause we got a little situation that needs to be taken care of. Looks like you going to be getting your feet wet quicker than expected," Rusty said trying to read Pop's facial expression.

"Some new niggas call themselves opening up on one of Fresh's corners. I'm going to need you and Pooh Bear to go over there and baseball bat them niggas down. Is that cool?"

"No, that won't be a problem," Pop answered. He and Pooh Bear went and hopped in a Ford Explorer with tinted windows.

"Some fools just don't learn," Pooh said nonchalantly. "I mean, I know these niggas knew they was opening up on someone else block."

Pop just sat in the passenger seat, staring out the window. He was in some deep shit and he knew it. This wasn't like robbing a Chinese delivery lady, this was a whole new ballgame, and he was dead in the middle of it.

"This a crazy way to make a living," Pop said, feeling the butterflies forming inside his stomach, but what other choices did he have? It was either do this or petty robberies. Instead of talking, he just sat back, visualizing how he was going to spend his money. First thing he planned on doing was getting up out of his mom's house. Once he accomplished that he planned on buying himself a car and saving the rest. But little did he know in this game things are much easier said than done.

Chapter Four

"It's about time you made some time for me," Amanda said as she sat in the Jacuzzi wiggling her toes.

"I told you I was going to make some time for you this week," Fresh said as the two relaxed in his condo out in Parkchester.

"Baby, come give me a massage," Amanda said, setting her glass of Grey Goose on the side of the tub.

"Chill, why you always trying to make me work?" he asked playfully.

"*Por favor papi*," Amanda begged in her Spanish accent, knowing when she spoke in Spanish Fresh would do anything she asked.

Five minutes into the massage Fresh heard his sidekick ringing.

"Who the fuck is this?" Fresh said out loud, flipping open his sidekick, noticing he had a new text message from Vanessa.

Baby, I miss you, I'm just sending you this message
'cause you were on my mind holla back

After he read the message, Fresh closed his sidekick and continued to massage Amanda's shoulders.

"Who was that?" she asked suspiciously.

"Business," he replied defensively.

"It better be," she warned. "*Pendejo.*" Amanda called him an asshole in Spanish because she knew that he couldn't understand her. It wasn't hard for him to get her back in the mood. He fondled her breasts and stuck his tongue down her throat and their antics resumed. He made her feel so good that she forgot they were ever interrupted.

While Fresh was kissing Amanda, he slipped his hand down in the water and began playing with her pussy.

"Mmm . . ." Amanda moaned softly as she bit on the bottom of Fresh's lip. She loved when he played with her pussy; something about that always just turned her on.

"I want to taste my pussy," Fresh whispered as he guided Amanda out of the water. He made her sit on the rim of the Jacuzzi with her legs spread apart. She watched as Fresh slowly slid down between her legs.

As soon as he was faced with her pussy, he quickly took both of her feet out of the water and placed them on his shoulders. Fresh knew he had been fuckin' up with Amanda lately and planned on doing whatever he had to do to get back in good. First he planted soft kisses all over her pussy and clit, then he let his tongue pick up where his kisses left off.

"Ah, *papi*," Amanda moaned as her body squirmed in pleasure. Seconds later, she wrapped her legs around the back of Fresh's neck as she began grinding her pussy on his tongue and face.

From the way Amanda moved and squirmed Fresh knew he was hitting her spot. He continued to lick her pussy, pretending his tongue belonged to a lizard.

Once Amanda came, she fought to get Fresh's face from between her legs. Her pussy was sensitive and she couldn't take it no more.

"Okay, okay, okay," she laughed as she finally removed his face from her pussy.

"What's the problem?" Fresh asked with a smile on his face as he stood up dripping wet.

"I thought you were a professional." He laughed purposely, standing directly in front of her so his hard dick was only inches away from her face.

"Oh, you talking shit, *papi?*" Amanda asked in her heavy accent as she grabbed Fresh's dick and began jerking it while she questioned him.

"What you want me to do to this dick? You want me to suck it?"

"Yeah, I want you to suck it," Fresh replied as if he was about to die.

"You want me to suck it like this?" Amanda asked as she took the whole thing into her mouth and held it there for seven seconds before releasing it, only to put the head back in her mouth while she roughly stroked his shaft with both of her hands.

"Damn," Fresh moaned as he grabbed a handful of Amanda's hair and began guiding her head with his hand. The way she was pulling and sucking on his dick, it took him no time to cum in her mouth.

"Oh my God, baby, you are the best," Fresh exclaimed as him and Amanda slid back into the Jacuzzi and just got their chill on.

"This is the easiest job in the world, all we have to do is baseball some clown down and get paid," Pooh Bear said, trying to keep his eyes on the road.

"How long you been working for Fresh?" Pop asked, trying to make conversation.

"About a year and a half now," Pooh answered, searching his memory.

"So what happens if we go to bat these clowns down and they strapped?"

"I never leave the house without my ratchet," Pooh answered, lifting up his shirt to reveal the handle of his .380. "You never know what might jump off, nah mean?"

"Yeah, I hear you," Pop answered, staring blankly out the window and suddenly feeling like the baseball bat in his hand wasn't enough.

When Pooh Bear pulled up on the block, two young kids had the block popping. The two youngsters hustled out in the open like what they were doing wasn't a crime.

"Yo, I'm going to keep these mu'fuckas still while you bat them clowns down," Pooh said as he pulled up directly in front of the kids.

"Don't y'all even think about moving," Pooh growled, aiming his .380 at the two kids.

"Yo, what's this all about?" one of the kids asked in a light whisper.

"Shut the fuck up," Pop spat as he swung the bat at the young kid's legs, dropping him instantly.

Once the kid hit the ground, Pop batted him down until he finally passed out. When he finished with the kid Pop quickly moved on to the next kid as a big crowd started to form.

"Chill, son, chill," the kid begged, but it did him no good. Pop swung the bat like he was Barry Bonds.

"A'ight, that's enough" Pooh said as he kneeled down and grabbed the kid by his shirt.

"This block belongs to Fresh, you understand?"

"Yes," the kid whispered through a pair of bloody lips and a bloody nose.

"If we have to come back again somebody is going to get killed," Pooh said in a icy tone as he punched the kid in the face one last time for good measure.

"You see, that wasn't so bad," Pooh chuckled as the two men hopped back in the truck and headed back to the projects.

"Before we go back to the hood, take me to Jimmy Jazz so I can pick up a few pieces," Pop said, pointing at his clothes.

"Yeah, you definitely need to do that. I wasn't going to say nothing but you look like a fuckin' bum," Pooh joked as he headed to 125th Street.

When Pop finally made it back to the projects, he headed straight upstairs so he could change his clothes.

"Yo, nobody better touch my shit, and I ain't playing," Pop warned, looking at his brothers and sister. He'd worked too hard for one of them trying to sneak and wear his shit.

Ten minutes later, Pop stepped out the building looking like a new man. He let his Red Monkey jeans sag on his Tims. Up top he wore a white T, with a Yankees fitted hat that covered his eyebrows.

When Pop stepped back outside, he noticed that he was walking different; his whole swagger had changed. He didn't know it, but having a pocketful of money boosted his ego.

"Okay, I see you looking like new money," Pooh said playfully.

"Come on, you know I had to step my game up, shit you was making me look bad, my nigga!" Pop said, giving Pooh a pound.

"I can dig it, but yo, we just have to look after these workers, make sure everything goes smoothly, look out for stickup kids, niggas trying to steal, and shit like that."

"This job is mad easy," Pop said.

"Nah, you just had an easy first day," Pooh assured him.

As the two men sat talking they noticed a dirty crackhead walk up.

"What up, Pooh? You think you can look out for me today?" the dirty bum asked.

"Lucky, I just hooked you up two days ago," Pooh reminded him.

"As much money as I bring in, I know you can toss me something," Lucky said, trying to give Pooh a pound.

Pooh looked at the dirty man's hand like it was infected with HIV "Nigga, didn't I just hook you up the other day? Damn, nigga, if you can't support your habit then you should get a new one or just quit," he told the crackhead.

"Come on, Pooh," Lucky begged. "You know my money is always straight, plus, my white friend is coming through later on with a pocketful of money, and you know I'm going to bring him here to spend with your peoples." As Lucky talked he scratched the nasty rash that was on his neck spreading down to his back.

"Here man, here," Pooh said, handing Lucky a ten-dollar bill. "Now get the fuck up out of here."

"Good looking, Pooh, you the best," Lucky said with a toothless smile, heading straight to one of the workers so he could get a blast.

"Would you believe this nigga had this whole hood on smash back in the day?" Pooh said, letting out a light chuckle.

"Get the fuck out of here," Pop stated in disbelief.

"Word, B. Nigga used to give me dollars when I was a youngin'. Crazy how shit turn out, right?" Pooh said, shaking his head.

"Yeah," Pop answered, looking at Lucky walk off to get his fix.

As Pop sat chilling, sitting on top of the bench, he saw Blondie from the Chinese restaurant coming his way.

"Yo, anybody got trees over here?" she asked, looking directly at Pop.

"Yeah, my man got it right there," he answered quickly, pointing to the young hustler sitting on top of the bench.

"A'ight, good looking," Blondie responded as she headed to cop some bud.

Yo, I'm feeling shorty for some reason, Pop thought as he kept his eyes on the young lady.

"Yo, ma, you live here?" he asked, approaching the pretty young thing.

"Yeah, I live right there in building two," she replied pointing.

"I'm going to have to chill with you one of these days," Pop said trying to sound extra smooth.

"That sounds cool to me," Blondie replied, licking her lips seductively.

"Yo, where your phone at?" Pop asked smoothly.

Blondie reached down in her purse and pulled out her phone. "You got me pulling out my phone, you better be about to give me your number," she said in a sexy voice.

"Don't take my shit if you not gonna use it," Pop said with a smile.

"I am going to call you," Blondie said, trying not to blush as she locked Pop's number inside her phone.

"What's good, you got a number?'

"Yeah, everybody calls me Nika."

"A'ight, I got you. My name is Pop, I'm going to call you later on tonight."

"A'ight, do that," Nika said throwing a little extra switch in her walk knowing Pop was watching.

"Yeah, I'm going to shagg that," Pop said looking at Nika's ass as she walked off.

"She must be new around here because I ain't never seen her before," Pooh stated as he noticed Fresh's Range Rover pull up to the side of the curb.

"Yo, Pop, let me holla at you for a minute," Fresh said, waving him over. "I heard you took care of business earlier," he stated.

"Business is business," Pop responded smoothly

"Come take a ride with me," Fresh said.

When Pop made it to the truck he noticed that Rusty was driving.

"Yo, you ever shot a gun before?" Fresh asked.

"Nah, I never could afford one," Pop replied.

Fresh smirked because he knew that it was probably for the best that Pop hadn't owned a gun. *This li'l nigga would've terrorized the entire projects if he had a burner on him.*

"Let me ask you a question. Do you like working for me?"

"It's okay I guess, the money is good," Pop answered honestly.

"Listen kid, I hired you 'cause I see that fire inside of you, the same fire I got in me, but don't get it twisted, li'l nigga. Out here in these streets you can lose your fuckin' life like this," Fresh said, snapping his fingers. "That's why Rusty is my personal bodyguard," he said as the truck came to a complete stop.

"Come on, li'l nigga, let me get you into beast mode," Fresh said, leading the two men into a warehouse.

When Pop stepped in the warehouse he saw a tableful of guns and a bunch of big wood boards hanging up.

"Yo, Rusty, teach this nigga how to shoot," Fresh ordered as he sat on the edge of the table and looked on.

When Pop felt that steel in the palm of his hand, he immediately felt a power rush; he felt untouchable with that gun in his hand.

"Just cock it back and pull the trigger," Rusty instructed, giving the young man a demonstration.

Pop did as he was told and watched fire spit out of the 9 mm once his finger squeezed the trigger.

As Fresh sat back watching Pop, he remembered what he had to go through when he first got in the game, all the nights he went with no sleep, all the times he wore the same outfit for weeks straight, all the shoot-outs and fistfights. Fresh snapped out of his daydream, glanced at the diamonds in his watch, and realized it was all worth it.

Nika sat on the couch daydreaming about Pop. She was feeling him ever since she saw him in the Chinese restaurant. Nika was loud, ghetto, and just didn't give a fuck, and on top of that she was a freak. She just hoped that Pop would be okay with her ways because she wasn't changing for no one. It was just something about Pop that made her want to know more about him and soon she would find out just what that was. She had gone outside, hoping she bumped into him when she went to go buy some weed. Now that she had gotten his number she felt much better.

"Who the fuck bought you new clothes?" Teresa asked with a busted lip as soon as Pop walked in the house.

"Not you, so don't worry about it," he shot back, not in the mood for her bullshit.

"Say it again so I can slap the living shit out of you," she yelled, getting all up in Pop's face.

"Yeah, that's what the fuck I thought," Teresa growled with her breath smelling like gin.

Instead of arguing with his mother, Pop just went into his room and closed the door.

"And don't be slamming no mu'fuckin' doors in my house!" Teresa yelled.

Once everybody in the house went to sleep Pop pulled out

his brand-new 9 mm that Fresh gave him and admired the chrome gun. Pop couldn't believe how his life was changing. Just the other day he was robbing the Chinese delivery lady, now four days later, he had over $500 dollars in his pocket. He knew none of this would be possible without Fresh, so he looked at Fresh like his ticket out of the hood. Pop was going to do whatever he had to do to make it out the hood, and especially out of his mother's crib, because she was really starting to work his nerves and he knew it would only be a matter of time before he snapped. So to avoid all that he knew he was going to have to move out and do it quick.

"Looks like it's just going to be me and you from now on," Pop said as he kissed his new gun, stuck it under his pillow, and went to sleep.

"That boy get on my goddamn nerves," Teresa huffed, sitting back on the couch. Every time she looked at Pop she saw his father's face, and that disgusted her. Every time she looked at her son it would always make her start to reminisce.

"Stop walking so fast, Tyrone," Teresa said, struggling to keep up with her man. "You know I can't walk but so fast in this snow especially while I'm pregnant."

"Bitch!" Tyrone with an attitude. "You better bring ya ass on. I don't got time to be waiting on ya fat ass. Nobody told you to come in the first place," he said, continuing to walk fast.

"Okay, I'm coming!" Teresa sucked her teeth, doing her best to keep up.

"You better not make me late," Tyrone warned. He was rushing to meet up with his side girlfriend, Sky. They had some credit-card scam business going on, and he was supposed to have met her ten minutes ago.

Teresa knew Tyrone was going out to handle business but she didn't trust her man around Sky. It was just something about the woman she just didn't like. Teresa knew that the two were fuckin' around; all she was missing was the proof. Before she got pregnant she had whipped Sky's ass at a local bar for being all up in Tyrone's face.

When Tyrone reached the corner he was happy to see Sky's car still there waiting for him. "My bad I'm late," Tyrone said as opened up the passenger door.

"That bitch ain't getting in my car," Sky said, snaking her neck. "She lucky I don't whip her ass."

"Beat who ass?" Teresa said, leaning down so Sky could see her face.

Sky quickly hopped out the car like she was going to do something, but then quickly turned her gaze on Tyrone. "She ain't getting in my car, so what you gon' do?" she asked, placing her hands on her hips.

"Yeah, what are you gonna do?" Teresa asked, placing her hands on her hips also.

"Let me talk to you for a second, baby," Tyrone said in a smooth tone as he pulled Teresa over to the side. "Listen, baby, I gotta get this money," he whispered.

"Well, you better think of another way 'cause I don't want you around that bitch," Teresa whispered back. "You know she wanna fuck you."

"I ain't thinking about all that, baby, we need this money," Tyrone said in a firm whisper. "Now let me do what I gotta do."

"Okay, baby," Teresa submitted. "You better not be out all night with this bitch either."

Tyrone gave her a look like she was insane. "Come on, baby, I'll be back before eight o'clock," he said as he slid in the passenger seat of Sky's car. Sky looked at Teresa and smirked before she pulled off.

Teresa watched her man ride off with the next bitch, while she had to walk home in the snow with tears in her eyes. For the entire walk home she cursed Tyrone out.

Later on that night Teresa dozed off on the couch. She woke up when she heard some keys fumbling around at her front door. She looked over at the clock on the wall that read 2:16 A.M.

Tyrone walked in the house with a handful of bags, laughing loudly with Sky on his heels. "Hey, baby, what you doing up? I thought you would be asleep by now," he said with a smirk on his face.

"Are you serious?" Teresa asked, getting up from her comfortable spot. "How dare you walk up in here at fuckin' two-twenty in the morning with a smile on your face," she began as she turned and faced Sky. "And what the fuck is you doing in my house?"

"Don't ask me ask ya man," Sky shot back.

"Oh, you think it's a game," Teresa said as she stormed into the kitchen. She returned holding a shiny kitchen knife. She tried to get at Sky but Tyrone blocked her path. "Move!"

"Put that knife down and stop acting stupid," Tyrone told her with a serious look on his face.

"Tyrone, you better get this bitch out my house before I do," Teresa said as she moved the couch out of the way.

"You know what?" Tyrone paused. "I ain't got time for this shit," he said as him and Sky made their exit.

"So you just gonna leave me just like that?" Teresa said, following them out into the hallway. "What about your child I'm carrying in my stomach?"

"Fuck you, and that baby probably ain't mine anyway," Tyrone yelled over his shoulder.

"So you leave your family to be with that bitch?" Teresa yelled at Tyrone's departing back. "Tyrone, Tyrone!" she yelled as she saw Tyrone and Sky disappear through the staircase door.

The beeping sound of the microwave snapped Teresa back into reality. "Fuck Tyrone, he can kiss my ass," she said to herself as she walked over to the microwave and retrieved her popcorn. Even though it was nineteen years later, Teresa still hated Pop's father to this day, and she was going to die feeling that way.

Chapter Five

Bamboo sat at his desk in his office, watching Fresh and Rusty pull up in his driveway.

"These surveillance cameras are lifesavers," Bamboo said to his bodyguard, King.

"Let me go let these clowns in," King said, walking toward the front door. "Gentlemen," King said, answering the door with his Uzi held tight under his armpit.

"King, what it do, my nigga?" Fresh responded as he and Rusty stepped foot inside the mansion.

"Bamboo is in his office," King said in a flat, unfriendly tone.

Rusty gave the big man a cold stare as he walked past. Rusty never liked King; it was something about him that bugged Rusty. All Fresh had to do was give him the word, and he would be more than happy to rock his ass to sleep.

"What's going on, baby?" Bamboo asked, giving Fresh and Rusty both a pound.

"You tell me, what's up with you raising your prices? We've been doing good business with you for a while, what's up?" Fresh stated.

"It's just a temporary thing. Shit is a little fucked-up on my side right now, just stick it out with me for a minute," Bamboo said nonchalantly.

"You saying stick it out with you like I'm not the one losing money," Fresh said, not understanding. "I mean, work with me, do something. Raise the prices on them other niggas. They not copping heavy like me anyway so what's the problem?"

"Fresh, in a month when this is all over I'll be sure to throw you something extra, a'ight?" Bamboo told him.

"Make sure you do that, 'cause I got a lot of people depending on me to come through, and you know when mu'fuckas pockets start getting short, people can't be held accountable for their actions," Fresh warned as he stood up to leave. "Yo, Pooh will be up here next week on his regular schedule," he stated plainly as he and Rusty headed for the door.

"No hard feelings," Bamboo yelled so Fresh could hear him. "I'ma take care of you."

"I'll believe it when I see it," Fresh said as he and Rusty made their exit.

"Hey, boss, why are you raising the price on Fresh? He's a good customer," King asked, unsure.

"Fuck that young punk," Bamboo snarled as he watched the monitors as Fresh pulled off his property. "He's lucky I don't triple the price on that faggot. I don't respect young hustlers; they think they know every goddamn thing when they don't know shit. I've been out here since the eighties when crack first started. Fuck Fresh—whatever I say the price is, he's just going to have to pay it point-blank. He need me, I don't need him. As soon as he try to get tough I'm going to cancel his fuckin' contract, simple as that," Bamboo chuckled, giving King a pound.

"But what we gonna do if Fresh finds a new connect?" King asked. "That's going to be mad money out of our pockets."

"Find a new connect where?" Bamboo asked, looking around.

"He ain't gonna be able to find a cheaper price anywhere else and if he does find it cheaper it won't be the same quality, so fuck him, he can kiss my ass."

"Why the fuck are we paying these high-ass prices for this garbage-ass work?" Rusty asked, confused.

"At the end of the month when we re-up we're going to take a package from Bamboo and not pay him shit," Fresh said, stopping at a red light. "I'm going to get ten bricks from him and just dead that clown."

"You know that's going to start a war, right?" Rusty stated plainly.

"I'm not even worried about that, B. My shoot-out record is twenty-two and oh, I'll take my chances, you dig?" Fresh paused. "As a matter of fact, fuck that—we ain't paying that nigga shit, if he want it he gon' have to take it in blood."

"I can dig it, you know I'm down for whatever," Rusty replied, giving Fresh a pound.

"Either ball hard or fall hard," Fresh said as he pulled up on the corner of Dyckman so he could get some raw piff.

Pop and Pooh stood in front of the building listening to Lucky try his hardest to sing an old school song.

"Okay, okay, that's enough," Pop said, interrupting Lucky in the middle of his song.

"I used to be one of the *Four Tops* back in the day," Lucky lied proudly.

"Nigga, you can't even spell *Four Tops*," Pop said, tired of listening to the dirty man's lies.

"Young blood, why you trying to disrespect me?" Lucky asked.

"Yo, just tell your wack-ass stories somewhere else," Pop said, not hiding his dislike for the man.

"Back in my day I would have knocked your young ass the fuck out," Lucky said coldly as he walked off.

"What!" Pop said as he quickly dug in the garbage until he found a bottle.

"Yo, chill," Pooh said, stopping Pop from throwing the bottle at the homeless man.

"That bum-ass nigga better watch his fuckin' mouth, before I break his jaw," Pop said watching the bum walk off still singing.

"You know he didn't mean anything by that shit," Pooh said, trying to calm Pop down.

"I'm about to get up out of here anyway—I got some pussy to get," Pop said, pulling out his cell phone.

Nika sat on the couch watching *The Wire* when she heard her phone ringing.

"Hello?" she answered innocently.

"Can I speak to Nika, please?"

"Yeah, it's me," she said in her sexiest voice.

"What's good? This Pop, you busy?"

"Nah, what's up? I thought you forgot about me," she responded.

"Nah, I just been a little busy, but I'm free now and I'm trying to see you, can you come to me or do I have to come to you?" Pop asked.

"I just got out the shower so you going to have to come see me," Nika replied flirtatiously.

"A'ight, bet, what's the apartment?"

"9E," Nika answered again in her sexy voice.

"I'll be there in about fifteen minutes," Pop said as he closed his cell phone.

"Okay, boo, I'll be waiting," Nika said right before the line went dead.

When Pop hung up he went straight to the corner store and bought a box of Wet n Wild before he headed toward Nika's building, hoping maybe tonight might be his lucky night.

Nika threw on some perfume as she heard somebody knocking on the door.

"What's up?" Nika asked, answering the door wearing nothing but a long T-shirt.

"Tryna see what's up with you," Pop answered as he stepped inside the apartment.

"I was just chilling, watching TV. Come sit down," Nika said, patting the cushion on the couch.

"Yeah, I think I saw this episode already," Pop said, moving in closer to her.

"Well, you better not tell me what's going to happen," Nika warned showing Pop her fist.

"Nah, I won't spoil it for you," Pop responded with a laugh and scooted even closer to her.

When Nika saw Pop moving closer to her she immediately went into panic mode.

If I give him some now he's going to think I'm a jump-off, then if I don't give him none he going to think I'm fronting. Damn, what should I do?

Before Nika could think of an answer she felt Pop's soft lips on her neck.

In a quick, smooth motion Pop slid Nika's shirt off and was happy when he saw that was the only thing she had on. He

immediately placed one of Nika's firm but soft breasts in his
mouth as his hands explored the rest of her body.

Nika let out a soft moan as she stuck her hand down Pop's
jeans and began stroking his penis with her hand, until it got
harder than a block of ice. All of her inhibitions went out of
the window when she felt the size of his dick. She didn't care
if he looked at her like a jump-off or not. She was wet and
needed him to handle his business.

"I want you to fuck the shit out of me," she whispered as
she laid back on the couch, spreading her legs open like the
Red Sea.

As Pop rolled the condom on he noticed Nika had two
piercings on the lips of her pussy.

"Oh, well," Pop said, shrugging his shoulders as he slowly
entered Nika's walls of heaven.

"Oh my God," Nika shouted as she dug her nails into Pop's
back, clawing away at his skin. She wrapped her legs around
his waist as Pop slowly slid in and out her at a nice pace. Once
Pop felt like he had broke Nika in, he quickly turned her
over on all fours. He pulled her hair as he watched his dick
disappear and reappear in and out of her juicy, wet pussy.

"Ooh," Nika moaned, loving every stroke. "Spread my ass
cheeks apart, daddy," she begged as she began throwing her
ass back.

"Damn," Pop groaned as he plunged in and out of her
sopping wet pussy.

"I wanna ride that dick," Nika said aggressively as she
forcefully pushed Pop down on the bed. She planted her feet
down on the bed as she bounced up and down on Pop's dick
like an animal.

Pop tried to last as long as he could, but Nika's pussy was so
wet, he couldn't help but cum faster than normal.

"Damn, I didn't know you were packing like that," Nika stated as she headed to the bathroom to clean herself up.

Pop just laid on the couch speechless, watching Nika's ass jiggle all the way to the bathroom.

"Yo, why do you have two earrings on ya pussy?" Pop asked, taking a sip of the orange juice he had just poured himself.

"Because I'm freaky like that," Nika said, letting out a light laugh before she continued. "A lot of times when I be walking, I just have an orgasm from the earrings rubbing up against my clit. Some people say I'm a freak but I say I'm just a girl that knows what she likes."

"Wow, that's some freaky shit, but if it works for you, then it works for me," Pop said, staring at Nika's naked body.

"I tell you how it is straight-up, plus I don't care what people think of me. It's what I think of myself that counts," Nika stated firmly as she sipped on her juice.

"I can dig it," Pop agreed.

For the rest of the night Pop and Nika sat up chitchatting and getting to know each other better.

The next morning Pop left Nika's crib while she was still sleeping. She was sleeping so peacefully that he didn't even bother to wake her up.

"I'll call her later," Pop said to himself as he hopped on the elevator and pressed the lobby button.

When Pop made it to the lobby he saw that there was nobody there except for an older-looking white man.

"Excuse me, sir, do you have change for a dollar?" Pop asked.

"Yeah, I think so," the white man responded as he dug into his pocket.

When the white man pulled four quarters out of his pocket, Pop already had his 9 mm pointed at his stomach.

"You know what time it is, old man," Pop said, snatching the white man's wallet from his back pocket along with his watch.

"Take anything you want, please just don't hurt me," the white man begged, throwing his hands up in surrender.

"Have a nice day, brother," Pop chuckled once he had all of the white man's belongings.

When he made it to the middle of the projects, Pooh was already playing the front of the building, watching the goings-on of Fresh's operation.

"What's good, my dude?" Pop said, giving Pooh a pound.

"I know you not just now getting back from shorty crib," Pooh said, fishing for some gossip.

"Yeah, I had a long night if you know what I mean," Pop replied as he playfully mushed Pooh.

"So what happened?" Pooh asked nosily.

"I shagged," Pop said nonchalantly, shrugging his shoulders. "You know, regular shit," he bragged as he saw Rusty coming down the path.

"What's good, my niggas?" Rusty asked, giving both men dap.

"I'm going to need you two to go to the Bronx and go see Pete for me, he owe Fresh some money. I don't care what y'all have to do just come back with that money," Rusty stated as he walked off.

Pooh and Pop knew Rusty didn't give a fuck about nothing—his nappy Afro and unshaved face told you to stay the fuck out of his way.

I wonder what he does with all his money, Pop wondered before Pooh interrupted his train of thought.

"Yo, I heard Tito is supposed to be coming home soon," Pooh stated as the two men hopped in the car to go handle Fresh's business.

"Who the fuck is Tito?" Pop asked, not really caring, but just being nosy.

"He was Fresh's second best soldier until he got locked up. That nigga is a straight-up fool, he's loud, rowdy, rude, and dangerous," Pooh said, trying to keep his eyes on the road and talk at the same time. "This Spanish cat is a straight-up loose cannon."

"Sounds like fun," Pop joked.

"It won't be no joking when that nigga touch down," Pooh claimed seriously.

"So who is this Pete guy?" Pop asked, changing the subject.

"Some clown that's always trying to be slick, always paying late, always got an excuse for why he ain't got the money," Pooh said pulling up on Pete's block.

Both men cocked back their pistols before they hopped out the car.

"I think this the apartment right here," Pooh said as he knocked on the door.

"Hey, what's up Pooh?" Pete said, extending his hand to give Pooh a pound.

"It's payday, my nigga," Pooh said, brushing past Pete, leaving him hanging.

"Give me a few days and I'll have it. This stupid-ass bitch fucked up a package but she working it off now," he told the two gunmen who stood in his living room.

"Mu'fucka, you already a week late," Pooh reminded him.

"I know, shit been mad slow around here lately," Pete said nervously as he lit a cigarette. "Give me two days tops and I'll have everything that's my—"

"Fuck all that, you got the money or not?" Pop growled, revealing his 9 mm.

"Chill, I told you I'm going to get it," Pete said, raising his brow. "Yo, Pooh, who is this new nigga?"

"This my man right here, that's all you need to know," Pooh told him. "You need to be worrying about getting that money."

"Tell this young wet-behind-the-ear mu'fucka that I'm good until next week," Pete boasted.

"Wet behind the ears?" Pop said, aiming his 9 mm at Pete's kneecap.

Pow!

The bullet ripped through Pete's knee.

"Aw, shit!" Pete screamed out in pain as he clutched his kneecap, watching the blood gush out.

"Last time I'm going to ask you," Pop said, placing the hot barrel to Pete's temple.

"Okay, okay, it's under the sink in the bathroom," Pete screamed out, still in pain, clutching his knee.

When Pop checked under the sink he found twenty stacks in a grocery bag.

"Grimy-ass nigga," Pop growled, kicking Pete on the side of his head.

"All we wanted was $15,000 stupid, now we taking all of it," Pop said, tossing Pooh the garbage bag full of money.

"Mu'fucka had twenty stacks back there," Pop said as he and Pooh made their exit, leaving Pete laid out on his living room floor leaking.

"Yo, go give Fresh that fifteen real quick," Pooh said as he doubled-parked in front of the warehouse.

When Pop made it to the front of the warehouse, Rusty was right there waiting for him.

"It's all there," Pop said, handing Rusty the garbage bag containing the money.

"Fresh would like to have a word with you," Rusty said as he led the way to Fresh's office.

"What's good with you, youngin'?" Fresh asked, sitting behind his desk.

"Ain't shit just out here getting this money," Pop responded, helping himself to a seat.

"I hear you been handling yourself well out there on the streets."

"I just try to do my part," Pop said.

"Bullshit, word on the streets is this nigga laying down order," Rusty cut in.

"Good, that's what we need; without order we will have disorder and disorder leads to conflict and we trying to do without conflict, you dig?" Fresh stated plainly.

"The reason I called you in here is because I like what you been doing on those streets. Keep it up and I might give you a promotion," Fresh told him.

"That's what's up," Pop said excitedly. "I appreciate it."

"And you the employee of the month," Rusty cut in again, slapping $500 dollars in Pop's hand.

"You family now, B. If you ever need something, all you have to do is ask, we take care of our own around here," Fresh said firmly.

"I feel you, looking for everything especially the opportunity," Pop said as he gave Fresh and Rusty both a pound, then made his exit.

"That little nigga got heart," Rusty said as he strapped on his bulletproof vest and loaded his 12-gauge shotgun.

"You ready?" Fresh asked.

"I'm always ready to take some of Bamboo's money," Rusty chuckled as the two men hopped in the all-black Denali and pulled off.

When Pop finally made it back to the projects, he wasn't quite ready to go upstairs so he just sat on the bench, enjoying the night air. As he sat on the bench chilling he saw Nika coming in his direction.

"Why you sitting over here all by yourself?" she asked.

"I was sitting here waiting for you, hoping you walked past," Pop joked on some lover-boy shit.

"You are such a liar," Nika said as she sat down next to Pop. "What you doing later on?"

"Nothing," Pop responded. "Why, what's good?"

"I was wondering if you wanted to keep me company later," Nika threw the question out there. She was afraid that he might not be interested. She hoped that Pop wasn't the type of dude who would hit it and quit it.

"No doubt we can definitely hook up later," he assured her.

Before Pop could say another word he saw Teresa coming his way looking like a bum.

She wore a stained-filled Newport T-shirt along with some orange shorts and a pair of blue run-down skippies to complete her outfit. Not to mention her hair looked like stir-fried shit.

"So is this where the fuck you be at all day long?" Teresa growled. "Sitting here on the bench not doing shit all day?"

"Why are you bothering me?" Pop huffed. Embarrassment filled him as he stared angrily at Teresa. He could feel Nika's eyes staring at him, but he didn't look her way.

"I ain't start to bothering you yet," Teresa said, putting her hands all up in Pop's face.

"Yo, back the fuck up out his face with all that," Nika said, hopping up off the bench.

"Bitch, I will tear your little ass up out here," Teresa shot back, trying to get her hands on the ghetto girl.

"Yo, chill," Pop said, holding his moms back.

"You better go hold that bitch before I whip the both of you. How dare you let her talk to your mother like that," Teresa said as she violently smacked Pop across his face, causing his hat to fly off.

"Fuck you do that for?" Pop yelled, ready to steal on his moms.

"You lucky that's all I did, now let me borrow ten dollars," Teresa said with her hand out.

"Nah, I ain't got it," Pop said, refusing to support his mother's bad habits.

"Why you lying for?" Teresa said loudly. "You think I don't know you out here selling drugs?"

"Fuck is you talking about?" Pop said with a disgusted look on his face. "I don't sell drugs."

"Yes, you do," Teresa snapped. "How else would you be able to get all those new fancy clothes you be wearing?"

"Whatever," Pop said, shaking his head from side to side. "You think you know everything, but you don't know shit."

"My bad, Pop, I didn't know that this was your mother," Nika said, feeling horrible inside. "I'm going home. Holla at me later. I'm sorry again," she said headed in the opposite direction.

"You always coming around with that bullshit, that's why I don't fuck wit' you like that," Pop said heatedly, pointing his finger at his mother.

"You better get your mu'fuckin' hand out my face before I break it," Teresa said with attitude, and placing her hands on her hips. "Yeah, you care more about that chickenhead than you care about your own mother."

"Yo, I'm out," Pop said as he walked off, leaving his mother standing there.

"Go ahead and chase that bitch, you won't give your own mother no money, but I bet you giving that bitch all your money, stupid ass. And you better not even think about bringing your black ass home tonight either," Teresa yelled, angry that Pop wouldn't give her no money.

"I'm sick of this bitch," Pop said to himself as he walked off. No matter what he did it was never good enough for his mother. He hated the fact that anytime she had a problem she took her anger out on him. There was no pleasing her, so Pop decided to stop trying.

Chapter Six

"Yeah, pull up right next to that nigga, Shawn," Fresh ordered, pointing in Shawn's direction.

"Yo, I'm going to take this nigga in the building. Wait five minutes before you come in," Fresh instructed as he hopped out of the car.

"My nigga, Shawn, what's good?" Fresh asked.

"You tell me, brother," Shawn shot back, trying to sound tough.

"Yo, Bamboo said you had something for me," Fresh said in a smooth, low-key tone.

"Nah, he ain't tell me no shit like that," Shawn said, pulling out his cell phone to verify what Fresh was saying.

"Keep your fuckin' hands where I can see them," Fresh said, placing his 9 mm to Shawn's ribs.

"Oh, it's like that? What you going to do when Bamboo finds out about this?" Shawn asked, angry that he had gotten caught slipping.

"Fuck Bamboo, I don't deal with problems—I make them," Fresh said, leading Shawn into the building.

"Y'all still keep the work on the fourth floor, right?" Fresh asked.

"Fuck you, Fresh, you going to have to kill me mu'fucka," Shawn said, wondering should he reach for the .22 that rested in his back pocket.

Before Shawn could make his move, Rusty walked in the building.

"What's good?" Rusty asked, holding his shotgun.

"This clown wants to be a tough guy," Fresh replied with a smirk on his face.

Without hesitation Rusty let the shotgun bark, sending Shawn skidding down the hallway.

"Yo, grab that work from the fourth floor so we can be out," Fresh ordered.

"Nothing personal, baby, just business," Fresh said, looking down at Shawn's dead body. Fresh quickly searched the dead man's pocket and stripped him of anything he had that was valuable.

Fresh knew that killing Shawn would send a message to not only Bamboo but to the streets also, and everybody knows the streets loved to talk.

"Sorry about that, my moms be bugging sometimes," Pop said, feeling like a complete idiot, as he stepped inside Nika's apartment. It didn't seem to matter what Pop did, his mother always found a way to spoil his day and embarrass him.

"That's okay, don't even worry about it," Nika said, feeling embarrassed for him. "I didn't know that was your mother; sorry for cursing at her," she apologized.

"It's all good. I'm about to start looking for a place anyway, 'cause I'm sick of her bullshit, and us in the same house ain't going to work," Pop told her honestly.

"So what's your plan?" Nika asked with a simple smile that let him know that she didn't look down on him or judge him for how he was living. She lived in the PJ's too so she could relate. Every apartment had a different ghetto story behind closed doors.

"What you mean?" Pop asked, confused.

"I mean what are you going to do until you find a crib?" Nika asked.

"I don't know. I guess stay in a hotel," Pop answered.

"Chill, you wilding. That's mad money going to waste. You might as well stay here until you find something," Nika suggested.

"Nah, I don't want to be all up in your space, and all that," he told her.

"It's cool, plus we can get to know each other better," Nika said, placing her hand on top of his hand.

"You sure about this?" Pop asked, making sure she was cool with the fact of him staying there.

"Yeah, it's all good, one hand washes the other and both wash the face, you know?" she stated.

"Thank you, I really appreciate it," Pop said gratefully.

"I think you know how you can thank me," Nika said, looking down at Pop's crotch, licking her lips.

"What's wrong? You seem so stressed-out." Amanda questioned as she gave Fresh an oil massage.

"I want you to move in here with me. I don't want you in those projects no more," he said.

"Why, is something wrong?" Amanda asked curiously.

"Nah, I just don't want you up in there no more," Fresh lied. "You know how you just get a funny feeling in your gut sometimes."

"Yeah, I know what you mean, boo, plus who would want their beautiful wife up in the PJ's all day?" Amanda said playfully.

Fresh knew soon he and Bamboo would more than likely end up going to war. And he didn't want Amanda getting caught up in no bullshit, and he definitely didn't want anybody trying to kidnap her, so to play it safe he just wanted Amanda out of harm's way.

"I think it is time we moved in together anyway," he told her.

"What about Melissa?" Amanda asked.

"Let her keep the place for herself, or she could move in with us if she want," Fresh said, taking a sip from his bottle of water. "Plus, I'm pretty sure your sister could use the privacy."

"Damn, I got a lot of shit that needs to be moved," she said, thinking about all of her valuable belongings.

"Let me worry about that, you just worry about passing your road test next week," Fresh joked. "How you twenty-three years old and still don't know how to drive?"

"Don't worry, I'm going to pass that test with flying colors, shit as bad as I want to drive I'm going to pass that test," Amanda said confidently as she watched Fresh take off his pants and head for the shower.

"Damn, I love that man," Amanda said to herself as she watched her man head for the shower.

When Fresh got out of the shower, he hopped on the bed and turned his TV to *SportsCenter*. As soon as he got ready to relax he heard his cell phone ringing.

"I know that nigga Fresh had something to do with this shit," Bamboo stated as he paced his living room back and forth.

"So how do you want to handle this, boss?" King asked, ready to put in some work.

"I'm not sure yet, first I have to see if it was him or not. Pass me my phone real quick," Bamboo said as he dialed Fresh's number.

"What's good? This Bamboo," he said in a calm manner.

"I know who this is," Fresh responded with ice in his tone.

"Yo, somebody murdered one of my mu'fuckin' workers and took my stash last night. I was wondering if you heard anything about that since I know you keep your ear to the streets?" Bamboo asked.

"Nah, B. I ain't heard shit," Fresh replied shortly.

"I don't know who could have done this, ain't nobody stupid enough to fuck with my shit, it must have been somebody who is not from around here," Bamboo said, trying to feel Fresh out.

"Yeah, probably," Fresh said as he yawned into the receiver.

"If you hear anything about this you make sure you let me know as soon as possible," Bamboo said in a threatening manner.

"I got you," Fresh said, hanging up in Bamboo's ear.

Bamboo looked at the receiver and his nostrils flared from the disrespect he had just been dealt. Sometimes it wasn't what a nigga did say, but what he didn't that determined his guilt and Bamboo was no fool.

"Yeah, it was Fresh and his peoples, I can tell by the way that clown was talking on the phone, mad nonchalant," Bamboo said, pouring himself a drink.

"It's time to put this fuckin' new jack in his place, yo call up my hit squad, I'm going to make an example out of that nigga that the streets won't soon forget."

Without hesitation King did as he was told.

"Nigga, it ain't no money like dope money," Pooh Bear said, counting his money outside on the bench, putting on a show for whoever was willing to watch.

"Yo, put that fuckin' money away, you don't know if we being watched or not," Pop said seriously.

"Nigga, pull your skirt down and have a little fun, I ain't doing nothing but enjoying life, you dig? You know tomorrow ain't promised," he reminded Pop.

Before Pop could respond he saw Lucky coming his way, drinking vitamin water.

"Nigga, why the fuck are you drinking a vitamin water?" Pop asked with a confused look on his face.

"Because it's good for my health," Lucky responded, flashing his rotten-toothed smile.

"Nigga, what the fuck is a vitamin water going to do for your health while you smoking crack, stupid?" Pop said as he bursted out laughing.

"Brother, I need all the vitamins I can get," Lucky chuckled as he walked off to go get his early-morning wake-up.

"Yo, that fool is crazy," Pop said as he noticed two uniform cops coming in his direction. "Yo, hold that down five-o coming."

Pooh quickly tossed his pocketknife and the little bit of weed in the grass before the officers walked up.

"Do you guys live in this building?" the white officer asked sourly.

"Yeah, why?" Pooh shot back. "What's the problem?"

"We got a complaint that two young guys were making a lot of noise in front of this building," the officer said, nervously placing his hand on his gun.

"Yo, the only reason why you fuckin' with us 'cause we black," Pop said disrespectfully, waving off the two cops. "Fuck outta here."

"Oh, we got a tough guy in the house, get up against the fuckin' wall, tough guy," the officer said, violently shoving the two suspects against the wall.

As the officers began to search the two men they noticed a large crowd started to form.

"Yo, that shit ain't right," shouted a black guy from in the crowd wearing a du-rag.

"Why don't y'all go to the white neighborhoods and do that shit," another young lady shouted.

"Y'all mu'fuckas lucky a crowd showed up," the white officer whispered in Pop's ear before him and his partner walked off with an attitude.

"Have a nice day, officers," Pooh yelled loud enough so the two officers could hear him. "Dickheads."

"I can't stand those dicks," Pop said, cracking open his Dutch Master, tossing the guts on the ground once the cops were out of eyesight.

"That's why I stay high, B. Them clowns just fucked up my whole day," Pop stated as he proceeded to roll up his blunt.

"Yo, come with me to building five real quick, I have to go check up on this clown that owe me some bread," Pooh said as he retrieved his weed and pocketknife from out the grass, then headed to the next building.

Before they could make it to the building, Pooh saw his victim walking out the building.

"Yo, Mike what's good you—got that money for me?" he asked way louder than he had to.

"I got you next week, I didn't get my check this week," Mike said, looking down at the ground, mad that he had bumped into the last person he wanted to see.

"Just like last week, right?" Pooh said, digging in his back pocket.

"Yo, Pooh, I promise I'm going to give you your money next week, you got my word," Mike said, looking at Pop giving him a private look that said Please help me.

Pop quickly broke eye contact with his former friend. He felt bad for Mike, but business is business, and this was all in a day's work.

"I know," Pooh said, flicking open the blade on his pocketknife.

Without hesitation he plunged the knife in and out of Mike's stomach three times, splattering blood all over the concrete.

"Have that for me next week B. Last time I'm going to tell you," Pooh said as he cleaned his knife off on Mike's shirt before he walked off.

Before Pop walked off he kicked Mike in the side of his face for good measure. "Punk mu'fucka."

"Y'all make the community look bad," an old lady said, shaking her head from a second-floor window. "Why don't y'all try doing something positive in the community instead of just trying to destroy and tear down the community."

"Shut up, old lady, before you be next," Pop growled, staring down the old lady. "Yo, I have to get out the hood tonight before I kill somebody," Pop said, taking a long drag from his blunt.

"We can go to the club tonight if you want," Pooh suggested.

"Yeah, that's cool. I think I need to be surrounded by some beautiful women tonight, know what I mean?"

"A'ight, bet, we going to hit up Club Spirit downtown. Fresh be in there every Friday, plus I heard it be jumping in there," Pooh said, doing his two-step.

"A'ight, I'm going home so I can go change I'ma meet you back here at eleven," Pop said as he headed home.

Fresh sat in his abandoned warehouse along with Rusty, counting piles of money.

"Yo, be on point tonight, just in case this clown Bamboo tries to make a move, smell me?" Fresh placed a rubber band over the neatly stacked money.

"You know I'm on it, I hope that nigga do make a move because I been dying to pop that nigga," Rusty joked, placing a rubber band on a stack of money.

"Yeah, I got a meeting with this Spanish cat next week, my man plugged me in, said this cat got the best coke on Broadway, so I'm going to go see what he working with, if he got that butter then that's going to be our new connect," Fresh said, sipping on his yak.

"A'ight, bet, that's what's up."

"I hope Spirit be popping tonight," Fresh said.

"You know it's popping every Friday," Rusty countered.

"Make sure you tell all the goons to strap up and be on standby just in case some shit jump off," Fresh ordered.

"I got you," Rusty said, placing all the money in two duffel bags.

"I can't wait until I hook this warehouse up," Fresh said, looking around. "In two weeks this place is going to look like new money, watch," Fresh said, looking at his vibrating Nextel.

"What's good, baby?" he answered.

"Hi, *papi*, when you coming home?" Amanda's voiced boomed on the other end of the phone.

"I won't be in until the morning; why, what's up?" he asked curiously.

"Get the fuck out of here, you must have been drinking tonight," Amanda said in her heavy accent.

"Chill, I'm going out with the guys tonight," he protested.

"*Tu loca?*" she exclaimed, asking if Fresh was crazy. "I'm going to the club too. I ain't going to be just sitting in the house all night by myself, plus Melissa was already going, so I was just going to hook up with her 'cause it's mad boring in the house."

"A'ight, a'ight, just don't be drinking too much *compren-der?*" Fresh used one of the few Spanish words he knew.

"Okay sexy, I'll see you in the club papi, bye," Amanda said, ending the conversation.

As Fresh sat on the phone with Amanda, Rusty sat back thinking back on how the two men met.

Rusty walked in the juvenile facility scared to death, but he knew if it came down to it he would get it on with anybody who tested him. He was the new kid in lockup and he knew how that shit went, but niggas had him all the way fucked-up if they thought that he was going to let them chump him. He didn't believe in that initiation bullshit. If somebody wanted to come at him wrong he would leave 'em bleeding.

As Rusty began to unpack his bag, two knuckleheads called themselves trying to extort him.

"Yo, what you got for me, fam?" the light-skinned kid asked, cracking his knuckles with his homeboy on his heels.

"Yo, my man, I ain't got nothing for you, go ahead with all that bullshit," Rusty said, waving the two kids off, not wanting to get into a scuffle his first day in the jail.

"What?" the other kid cut in. "Yo, fam, play the bathroom," the kid said as he and his partner headed to the bathroom.

Rusty tied his sneakers up real tight and took a deep breath before he headed to the bathroom. He didn't want to fight, he just wanted to do his time and get it over with but the two punks were already trying to make his stay more uncomfortable than it already was.

Once Rusty stepped foot in the bathroom it was no talking, he walked straight up to the light-skinned kid and started swinging like a madman. His first two punches connected with the light-skinned kid's jaw, making a loud clapping sound.

Within seconds Rusty felt his opponent's partner punching him in the back of his head. He felt punches coming from every angle as he quickly turned his attention toward the partner.

They finally got Rusty on the floor, and started viciously kicking him in his ribs and back.

Rusty thought it was over for him until Fresh came to his rescue.

Fresh pulled out a sock with three bars of soap inside and beat the two kids like they stole something valuable from him and his mother. He swung the soap in a sock like a violent pair of nunchakus until both of the young kids were laid out on the bathroom floor leaking. Once he finished handling his business, Fresh quickly handed the bloody sock to one of his partners to get rid of the evidence of a weapon.

"Yo, you a'ight, B?" Fresh asked, helping Rusty back to his feet.

"Yeah, good looking, them bitch-ass niggas had to jump me because they knew they couldn't beat me one-on-one," Rusty said, spitting out blood.

"Yeah, these clowns tried to do the same shit to me when I first got here," Fresh said, kicking the light-skinned kid in the face one last time.

"Yo, nigga, you ready to go?"

"Huh?" Rusty asked, snapping out of his daydream.

"Nigga, you ready to go to the club and see some beautiful women?"

"If the ass is round you know I'm down," Rusty joked as they left the warehouse on their way to the club.

***

"Damn, girl, you wearing them jeans," Amanda teased her sister.

"You know I does this," Melissa joked, pretending she was walking down the runway.

"Girl, when you going to find you a man?"

"All the men I come across all act like little boys," Melissa said, fixing her makeup. "But when I do find a man, he going to be the perfect man," she chuckled, giving her sister a high five. "Now you know that skirt is too short, Fresh is going to be flipping when he see you."

"I am a grown-ass woman, plus I can't help it that I'm sexy," Amanda said, strapping up her three-inch heels. "Don't worry about my man, worry about trying to get you a man."

"Don't worry, it won't be long," Melissa assured her older sister.

When the two sisters stepped outside, they turned the heads of every man in sight.

"*Muy bien, mami,*" crackhead Lucky said as he walked past the two Spanish divas.

"I hate that crackhead, he's always staring at me," Melissa said, frowning up her face.

"Leave that junkie alone, he ain't bothering nobody," Amanda said, flagging down a cab. "Let's just have us a good night," she said as the two hopped in the cab.

"Let's pray these fools up in this club act like they got some sense tonight," Melissa said as the cab pulled off, taking them to their destination.

"Damn, look at all these hoes," Pooh said as he slowly cruised past the club.

"Yo, that line is around the fuckin' corner," Pop stated, throwing a piece of Winter fresh in his mouth.

"Come on let's get up in here," Pooh said as they placed their guns under their seats and headed inside the club.

"What's good, my dude?" Pooh said, giving the bouncer a pound and slipping fifty dollars in his hand.

"How many you got with you tonight?" the big bouncer asked, discreetly stuffing the bill in his pocket.

"Just me and my man right here," Pooh said as he and Pop bypassed the line and entered the joint.

When Pop stepped foot inside the club he almost went crazy. This was his first time ever going to the club—he wasn't even old enough to get in yet—but he was connected now.

Pop was only eighteen, but that night he felt like he was over twenty-one and loved every minute of it.

Pop watched as Pooh gave dap to the people he knew. Pop could tell that most of the guys were drug dealers and most of the girls were gold diggers looking for a quick come-up. Almost every woman was dressed in something skimpy or dressed like a prostitute in order to catch the eye of a baller. As Pop and Pooh walked through the crowded club, they saw Fresh waving them over to his VIP section.

"My niggas, glad y'all could make it," Fresh said, giving both men pounds.

"Had to get out the hood for a minute," Pop said, accepting the drink that Rusty was handing him.

"If you stay in the hood too long it will drive you crazy," Fresh replied as he noticed Amanda and Melissa walk up in the club.

"Come over here so I can holla at y'all for a second," Fresh said as the duo took a seat on the couch.

"I'm going to need you two to take care of something for me tomorrow, something serious," he said.

"Whatever it is I'm sure we can handle it," Pop stated as he killed his drink.

"One of my lieutenants got himself mixed up in a murder charge," Fresh whispered in a huddle.

"So what, you need us to take out the witness?" Pooh joked.

"That's exactly what I need y'all to do," Fresh said seriously before he continued. "Some lady in her early thirties." Fresh handed Pooh a photo of the woman.

"I'm missing out of a lot of money while my man is sitting up on Rikers Island. There's no way this woman can testify," Fresh said with seriousness in his voice.

"Is she in protective custody?" Pop asked curiously.

"Nah, not that I know of," Fresh responded.

"Don't worry, we'll take care of it, but not tonight, my nigga," Pooh said as he got up and headed to the dance floor.

"Enjoy the rest of your night, get you one of these fine-ass bitches up in here," Fresh chuckled as Amanda walked up right on time.

Pop hit the dance floor and saw Pooh getting his freak on with some thick, dark-skinned chick. Pooh was a straight-up animal while he was on the dance floor; he and the dark-skinned chick practically had sex with their clothes on for three songs straight.

Pop stood there watching everybody have a good time until he saw the Spanish girl of his dreams. Instantly Pop's stomach caught butterflies. He knew if he was ever going to holla at the Spanish girl now was the perfect time.

What the fuck are you waiting for? The worst thing she could say is no, Pop said to himself as he made his way over to the sexy woman.

As Pop got closer he noticed that the Spanish girl looked even prettier on a club night.

Melissa stood by the bar doing her two-step when the ugliest guy in the world approached her.

"Hey, baby you wanna dance?" the ugly man asked, grabbing Melissa's wrist, moving his hips to the beat.

"No, thank you," she said politely, but the man still held on to her wrist.

"Come on, ma, don't act like that, let's try this again," he said, still moving his hips to the beat. "Would you like to dance?"

"Not with you," Melissa said, snatching her wrist out of the ugly man's grip.

"Well, fuck you then, bitch," the ugly man spat as he disappeared in the crowd.

"What's good, ma, you look like you can use a drink," Pop said, looking at his dream girl in the eyes.

"I sure can," she replied, looking the young stud up and down.

"I'm Pop," he said, extending his hand.

"I'm Melissa. It's nice to meet you, Pop," she replied with a gorgeous smile.

"What you drinking, ma?" he asked as he pulled a nice-sized knot out of his pocket.

"I'll have a Long Island iced tea," she answered.

"Yo, let me get two Long Islands," Pop yelled to the bartender over the loud music as he placed a big face on the bar top.

"Thank you," Melissa said, accepting the drink.

Before Pop could start spitting his game the DJ started mixing an old Jim Jones cut. "We fly high," came blaring through the speakers and even though it was old it still got the club jumping. The entire club went crazy.

"This is my song," Melissa said as she grabbed Pop's hand and led him to the dance floor. Once on the dance floor Melissa dropped to the floor and came back up, placing her fat ass on Pop's crotch, never missing a beat. When Pop looked down he couldn't believe his eyes, he couldn't believe whose ass was rubbing up against him. But it was true: Pop was an up-and-coming street star, and from now on he would only have the finer things in life.

"Who's that nigga Melissa is all up on like that?" Amanda asked, pointing in her sister's direction.

"Oh, that's my nigga, Pop," Fresh answered.

"He ain't a rapist or no shit like that right?" she asked, being overprotective of her sister.

"Nah, he cool peoples," Fresh assured his woman.

"Yo, what you doing after the club?" Pop asked, hoping the woman didn't have no plans.

"Nothing, why what's up?" Melissa asked, happy 'cause she really wasn't ready to go home.

"I'm going to grab something to eat; I was wondering if you would join me," Pop asked.

"Of course I will," Melissa said, smiling from ear to ear. "I'm starving."

"A'ight, let's go chill over in the VIP section until you ready to be out," Pop said as he put his hand on her lower back and guided her through the crowd.

When Pop and Melissa stepped in the VIP section all eyes were on them.

Even Rusty couldn't believe that Pop had pulled it off, 'cause back in the day he even tried to holla at Melissa, but had failed miserably.

Pop and Melissa sat sipping on some champagne as they got to know each other better. While everybody was enjoying themselves, Rusty stood up watching over the crowd, making sure no haters were feeling froggy.

"Yo, y'all ready to be out?" Fresh asked his crew once the party started to die down.

"I'm waiting on y'all," Pop answered, feeling a little tipsy.

Everybody left the club in packs and met up in the parking lot.

"Yo, we are all going to meet up at the small diner a couple of blocks away, a'ight?" Fresh ordered.

"My sister is going to ride with me, I'll meet you at the diner," Melissa said as she kissed Pop on the cheek.

"A'ight, say no more," Pop replied as he slid in the passenger seat of Pooh's whip.

"Yo, I'm going to check you when you get to the diner," Fresh said as he playfully slapped Amanda on her butt.

"Don't start nothing you can't finish out here, *papi*," Amanda shot back as she slid in the passenger seat of her sister's ride. Everyone filed into a vehicle and they departed.

"Yo, it was mad jump-offs up in there," Rusty said, stopping at the red light.

"Yeah, it was poppin' in that joint," Fresh responded, checking the text message he just received from Vanessa.

"I'm hungrier than a mu'fucka," Rusty said as a minivan cut right in front of him. Rusty saw the doors of the minivan open up and his eyes bucked in surprise.

"Watch out, Fresh, it's a hit!" Rusty yelled as he threw the Navigator in reverse.

Before Rusty could step on the gas, another minivan stopped right behind the Navigator, boxing them in.

Fresh pulled out his .40-caliber, but he was a bit too slow. He quickly ducked down as the bullets started raining in the SUV.

"Oh, shit, that's Fresh and Rusty," Pop yelled, retrieving his 9 mm from under his seat.

Pooh quickly pulled up a couple of feet behind the mini-van.

Immediately, Pop sprang from the passenger seat, letting

off four thunderous shots. Two of the four shots took out two of the gunmen. Once the other gunman saw Pop letting off shots, they immediately turned their attention to Pooh's truck.

Pooh and Pop quickly took cover behind the truck as the gunmen's bullets made loud pinging noises as they connected with the truck. When Rusty noticed the bullets stop raining, he immediately pulled out his Dessert Eagle and pulled the trigger at the first gunman he saw.

As Rusty went to hop out the truck he noticed that Fresh was bleeding.

"Stay down, my nigga," Rusty yelled as he slid out the truck and continued to let his Desert Eagle bark.

Once the gunmen saw that the shoot out was no longer one-sided, they desperately hopped back in their vans and fled the scene.

"Yo, Pop, I need some help over here—Fresh got hit," Rusty yelled, waving Pop over.

When Pop made it over to the truck he noticed that it was blood everywhere.

"He isn't hit bad is he?" Pop asked, scared to look.

"Nah, I'm good, B," Fresh slurred, clutching his shoulder.

"Where you hit at?" Rusty asked.

"I took one in the shoulder, hand, and my thigh," Fresh responded as he saw Melissa's car pull up to the scene.

"Oh my God!" Amanda screamed as she rushed over to the truck.

"*Papi*, are you okay?"

"Yeah, I'm good baby, it's only a flesh wound," Fresh lied as he heard sirens getting louder and louder.

"Yo, Rusty, get rid of these hammers before the police get here," Fresh instructed, still trying to lead his squad while he was down.

Rusty quickly snatched Fresh's .40-caliber from his waistband and handed both guns to Melissa.

"Get these out of here," Rusty ordered sharply.

"I got you," she responded as she tossed the guns in her trunk.

"Pop, give me your gun too," Melissa said, not wanting Pop to get in any trouble.

Once she had all the guns, she quickly hopped in her car and rode right past the police as if nothing ever happened. Pop smirked, thinking how cool she acted under pressure. There were no tears or questions. *I just might have found my Bonnie,* he thought.

Thirty seconds later the streets were flooded with police cars and flashing lights. They made sure they questioned every innocent bystander in sight only to hear everyone give the same answer: "I didn't see or know nothing."

As each minute passed more people arrived to see what was going on.

The paramedics placed Fresh on the stretcher and began to roll him to the ambulance.

As Fresh laid on the stretcher, he stared out at the sea of black faces watching him. In his mind he knew who had done this to him, now it was time to retaliate; Bamboo had to pay for this one. Fresh couldn't help but be embarrassed as he was getting rolled to the ambulance.

"It's all part of the game," Fresh said to himself as the ambulance doors closed.

Chapter Seven

Pop woke up the next day still thinking about what had happened to Fresh.

It's crazy how fast shit can get fucked-up, Pop thought to himself as he saw a head peek through the door.

"Hey, baby, I made you some breakfast," Nika whispered as she entered the room.

"Thank you, baby," Pop said, finally sitting up.

"You still thinking about what happened last night?" Nika asked, already knowing the answer.

"Yeah," he began quietly. "It's just crazy how fast that shit popped off."

"You just lucky that it wasn't you in the back of that ambulance, you got a lot to be grateful about," she reminded him.

"Yeah, I know," he said, rubbing his chin.

"Cheer up, baby, it always could be worst. Fresh is still alive, right?" Nika stated cheerfully as she got undressed.

"I guess you right," Pop said as he watched Nika's fat ass jiggle as she walked to the bathroom to take a shower.

"Yo, hurry up because we still have to meet this car dealer nigga in an hour," Pop yelled loud enough for her to hear him.

Pop was so excited he couldn't sit still. Rusty had set him up with the car dealer that him and Fresh always dealt with, so Pop didn't have to show pay stubs and go through all that other bullshit . . . just pay, sign, and be out.

When Pop and Nika stepped foot on the car lot they felt like little kids in a candy store.

"Damn, look at that Lex," Nika said, pointing to a beautiful dark red vehicle.

"You must be Pop," the Italian car dealer stated.

"Yeah, that's me," Pop answered, shaking the Italian man's hand.

"Take your time, when you're ready I'll be in my office," the Italian salesman said before he disappeared inside the small office.

"Which one should I pick, the Magnum or the Charger?" Pop asked.

"They both hot if you ask me," Nika stated, not being much help at all.

"Fuck that, I'm going to roll with that all-black Dodge Magnum with the chrome rims and tinted windows," Pop said as he made his way to the office.

"Yo, how much for that Magnum out there with the rims and tinted windows?" he asked.

"Since you roll with Fresh just give me twenty-five stacks," the Italian said nonchalantly.

Pop had a huge decision to make being that he only had $26,000 dollars to his name. It was either get the car and be broke, or don't get the car and have money.

Pop pulled out of the dealer's lot on top of the world; he had a new car and a bad bitch sitting in the passenger seat.

Pop turned up the volume on his new stereo, blasting, "Hey, Papi," by Jay-Z. He loved the attention he was getting in his new ride.

He was getting addicted to the fast life and was loving every second of it.

"Yo, I'm going to be back a little later, I have to go take care of some business real quick, a'ight?" he told Nika, as he dropped her off infront of her building.

"A'ight, be careful baby," Nika said as she kissed Pop on the cheek and headed upstairs.

Once Nika was gone, Pop couldn't wait to get his floss on and show Pooh his new ride.

Pop pulled up on the avenue and double-parked, blasting his music.

When Pooh saw Pop hop out of the Magnum he couldn't believe it.

"Oh, shit, that's what I'm talking about, B," Pooh said, giving Pop a pound. "That's a good look for you right there my dude."

"Come on, Pooh, you already know how I do. Nothing but the finer things in life for me from now on. Smell me?" Pop boasted.

"I can definitely dig it," Pooh said as he admired his friend's new car before he quickly changed the subject.

"Yo, you know we have to go take care of that witness in a few hours right?" Pooh reminded.

"Fuck it we can do it now if you want," Pop said, shrugging his shoulders.

"Bet we out," Pooh said as they made their way toward the vehicle.

The whole time Pooh and Pop had their little conversation, they never realized that they were being watched.

Two detectives stood in an apartment above the bodega on the corner taking pictures of the two suspects.

"It's only a matter of time before we have all the evidence we need to put these idiots away for a long time," the Chinese detective stated to his partner.

"Yeah, these guys been doing the same routine for the past six months," his partner added.

"Like I said it's only going to be a matter of time, I guarantee you."

"Yeah, that's the building right there," Pooh said as he pulled over and doubled-parked his Ford Explorer.

"I got shit to do tonight, Pooh, so let's make this as quick as possible," Pop stated as he loaded his .40-caliber.

"I got you, partner," Pooh responded as the two men exited the vehicle.

Once they reached the apartment, both men quickly drew their weapons. On the count of three, Pooh turned and attempted to kick in the door. He failed on the first try but was successful on the second.

"Nobody fuckin' move," Pop yelled as he entered the apartment first, followed by Pooh.

When the two men bum-rushed the apartment they were both caught off guard. Pooh and Pop stood shocked as they saw the black police officer who was suppose to be protecting the witness having wild sex with the white woman.

"Hey, hold on brothers, y'all don't have to do this," the black officer begged.

Without a trace of emotion Pooh raised his pistol and shot the officer in his head, sending pieces of his face splattering all over the white woman.

"Please don't kill me I won't testify, I promise," she begged. "Wait, I got money if that's what y'all want," the white woman begged, her voice changing to a nagging, whining tone.

"How much money you got?" Pop asked curiously.

"I got fifteen thousand in my pocketbook," the white

woman answered, pointing to her pocketbook lying on the kitchen table.

Pop went and checked the woman's pocketbook, while Pooh kept his pistol trained at the white woman's head.

Pop tossed everything out of the woman's pocketbook until he found a envelope full of one-hundred dollar bills. He quickly stuffed the envelope in his back pocket, walked up to the witness, and shot her in the head.

"Come on, we out," Pop stated as they made their exit.

When Pop stepped out of the building he glanced down the block to see if the gunshots had drawn any attention. Once the coast was clear the two gunmen hopped in the Ford Explorer and burned rubber.

"Yo, here's your cut," Pop said, handing Pooh $7,500 dollars.

"Good looking," Pooh countered as he stuffed the money in the inside pocket of his jacket. "We need jobs like this more often."

"I know that's right," Pop responded quickly.

"This the best job in the world," Pooh stated as he pulled up in front of Fresh's warehouse.

"What's going on, gentlemen?" Rusty asked, counting a large stack of money.

"Did y'all take care of that witness yet?" Rusty asked.

"Of course we did," Pop answered confidently.

"That's what I'm talking about," Rusty said, tossing Pop the stack of money he was counting. "Make sure y'all split that."

"A'ight, I got you but what's up with Fresh?" Pop asked.

"He doing okay, word on the streets is Bamboo paid for that hit, so I'm going to round up a few soldiers and pay that clown a little visit tomorrow, you dig?"

"That's what I'm talking about," Pop said, ready to retaliate.

"Y'all niggas go get some rest, 'cause it's on and poppin' tomorrow" Rusty said, walking the two men to the door.

"That nigga Bamboo going to get his cap peeled," Pooh said as he hopped on the FDR highway.

Pooh sat running his mouth while Pop had his mind on something else.

"You heard me, nigga?"

"Huh?" Pop asked, snapping out of his deep thoughts.

"Oh, yeah, Bamboo is a goner," Pop stated as he pulled out his Nextel and started dialing numbers.

Ever since the other night Melissa couldn't help but think about anything or anybody but Pop. She just loved how he walked and carried himself, not to mention his swag. Usually, Melissa didn't deal with guys that were in the street game, which was a turnoff for her, but with Pop it was different. It seemed like instead of turning her off, his gansta style was turning her on.

As Melissa lay down to go to sleep she heard her cell phone ringing. When she looked at the caller ID, she didn't recognize the number.

"Hello," she answered.

"Can I speak to Melissa please?"

"Speaking," she answered, wondering who was calling.

"What's good, this Pop."

"Hey, Pop, I was just thinking about you," she said as she sat up and cradled the phone with her shoulder and ear.

"Word? That's funny because I was just thinking about you too, what you getting into tonight?" Pop asked, his voice low and mysterious.

"I was about to go to sleep," she responded.

"Sleep? Chill out with all that. Get dressed, I'm about to come scoop you up," he told her.

"You bugging, I have to go to school in the morning," Melissa answered quickly as she glanced at the clock, noticing that it was close to midnight.

"I'm already right around the corner, plus I ain't going to keep you out all night you dig? Hurry up I'm going to be waiting for you in front of your building," he stated, leaving her no room to say no.

"A'ight, I'll be right down," Melissa said, closing her cell phone.

Melissa quickly got undressed and hopped in the shower. Twenty minutes later, she stepped out her building looking brand new.

As she headed to the corner she didn't see Pop, but when she saw the Magnum sitting on chrome she knew it had to be him.

"Hey, what's up?" Melissa asked, sliding in the passenger seat.

"Chilling, ma, I just wanted to see your pretty face before the night was over," Pop replied honestly.

"Thank you; that is so sweet," she said, blushing. "So what did you have in mind?"

"Oh, nothing special because I know you got school in the morning," Pop said, making the engine come to life. "Yo, you hungry?" he asked, taking a long drag off the piff he was smoking.

"A little bit," Melissa answered.

"A'ight, I'm going to take you to my favorite spot," he told her.

Ten minutes later, Pop double-parked in front of Popeyes fried chicken.

"Come on, we out," Pop said, exiting the vehicle.

"You just going to leave your car doubled-parked like that?"

Pop shrugged his shoulders, then answered, "Yeah, why not? Nigga know who this car belongs to, plus they know better than to touch my wheels," he bragged, trying extra-hard to impress her.

Pop and Melissa sat in Popeyes eating and getting to know each other better. Melissa was really enjoying herself, not only was Pop a cutie but he was also funny and cool to be around. She couldn't remember the last time she had liked a guy so much.

As the two sat talking, he wondered if he wasn't getting money, would he be able to pull a girl like Melissa. A few months ago she didn't even know he existed.

"What are you thinking about?" Melissa asked when she saw Pop staring off into space looking like he had something heavy on his mind.

"How beautiful you are," Pop answered, snapping out of his daydream.

"That was a nice comeback," she said, letting out a light chuckle.

After the two finished eating, Pop and Melissa just sat in the car and talked for a few hours.

"Yo, I want to thank you for what you did for me the other day," he said, placing his hand on her thigh.

"You don't have to thank me for that, you know I don't want to see nothing bad happen to you, plus jail is no place for a black man," she reminded him.

"You definitely right about that," Pop agreed as he leaned over and kissed Melissa. The kiss caught her off guard, but she remained cool until he started feeling on her breast.

Instantly Melissa felt her pussy getting soaking wet; as bad as she wanted the dick she had to remain cool.

"Hold on I think we moving a little too fast," Melissa said, removing Pop's hands from her breast. In all reality she just didn't want to seem like a jump-off or a slide, because the truth was she wanted Pop more than he wanted her.

"Plus, it's getting late," she continued, "and I got school in the morning, sweetheart."

"I respect that," Pop said, making the engine come back to life.

The two chitchatted until they reached the front of Melissa's building.

"Damn, these bum-ass niggas is still outside," Melissa stated, talking about the local thugs that stood in front of her building. "All they do is roll dice all day, drink forty ounces, and talk shit all night long."

"Yeah, but that's every project," Pop said, checking out Melissa's ass as she slid out the vehicle.

"Maybe next time I'll invite you upstairs," she said, sticking her head in the passenger window.

"That would be nice," Pop countered smoothly.

"Maybe," Melissa said as she turned and headed to her building, throwing a little bit of extra switch on her walk.

"Damn, shorty thicker than a Snickers bar son," one of the thugs said, unconcerned about how his words would affect the woman walking in the building.

"Damn, her ass is fat," his drunk partner cut in. "You wanna do something strange for some change?" The two thugs laughed loudly, not caring about the feelings of the woman who they spoke of.

"Why don't y'all get a fuckin' life?" Melissa said angrily as she entered the building. So happy that the elevator was right there, she just pressed her floor repeatedly until the door finally closed and took her upstairs.

Once Pop was sure that Melissa had made it inside the

building, he quickly hopped out his car and headed in the next building.

Pop was in love with two women. He knew it was wrong, but what was he supposed to do? He had feelings for both women. Nika was a down-ass chick who was down for him despite where he came from and Melissa was the chick that he had dreamed of bagging. She was a necessity for every hood nigga. She was the showpiece and the bad bitch that he needed on his arm. She symbolized his arrival. He had a special place in his heart for both ladies. He hoped he never had to choose.

Chapter Eight

"Fresh, why don't you put a smile on that handsome face of yours?" Amanda said, trying to cheer her man up.

"I ain't got a fuckin' thing to be smiling about right now," he said, pausing for a moment, "and I'm damn sure not happy to be sitting up in this fuckin' hospital."

"Fresh, all you doing is thinking about all the negative shit, why don't you start thinking about the positive shit?"

"There ain't a damn thing positive about lying up in a hospital bed," he growled.

Fresh was about to continue but held onto the rest of his words when he saw the nurse come in carrying a whole bunch of flowers and balloons.

"I'm sorry if I disturbed you," the nurse said, placing the flowers and balloons on the table in the corner of the room. "Can I get you anything before I go?" she asked innocently.

"No, thank you, I'm fine," Fresh answered, knowing he was in big trouble.

As soon as the nurse stepped out of the room Amanda was all over him. "Who the fuck is sending you flowers and shit?" she asked with fire in her voice.

"How the fuck would I know?" Fresh said, already knowing shit was about to hit the fan.

"You don't know? Okay, why don't we just find out," Amanda growled, snatching the card out of the flowers.

"I'm sorry I couldn't make it, baby," Amanda said, making sure she dragged out the words before she finished reading the card. *"I hope you get well soon, love Vanessa."*

"Who the fuck is Vanessa?" she asked, placing the card inches away from Fresh's face so he could get a good look at it.

Fresh didn't answer, instead, he just shook his head no. "I don't know who that is."

"Now you just going to play stupid, right?"Amanda asked as fire blazed in her eyes and a frog caught in her throat.

"Yo, I don't know who the fuck that is. What you want me to do?" Fresh said, lying with a straight face.

"Fuckin' liar! I look stupid to you, mu'fucka?" Amanda asked, trying to fight back the tears. "Trust and believe ain't no bitch sending you no flowers and balloons out the blue—that bitch is sending you shit for a reason."

"I told you I don't know who the fuck that is," Fresh answered, quickly getting an attitude.

"Bullshit, Fresh! *Con quien estas hablando?*" Amanda went off in Spanish, demanding to know who Fresh was talking to as she placed her hands on her hips. "Don't fuckin' play with me, Fresh, 'cause you know I don't be with all that bullshit," she warned.

Once Fresh heard Amanda start talking in Spanish he knew she was heated. "Listen, baby, calm down for a second, I told you I don't know no fuckin' Vanessa," he lied again.

"Well, she sure as hell know who you are," Amanda said, rolling her eyes. "Now explain."

"Ain't nothing to explain," Fresh said. "I don't know who sent them shits."

"Fuck you, Fresh, you a real piece of shit you know that? I'm out of here. You about to lose a good thing. *Perdedor!*" Amanda said, calling him a loser as she stormed out of the room.

"Damn," Fresh said, looking up at the ceiling. he didn't know what the fuck Amanda was saying, but he knew he had just fucked-up big time. He figured Amanda would come back eventually, or so he thought.

"Listen, I don't want no bullshitting when we get in there, we going to smoke everybody in the mu'fuckin' house pointblank," Rusty stated as the rest of the crew loaded their weapons. Everybody in the crew wore all black like Rusty had instructed.

"I'm laying something down tonight!" Pooh said, admiring the shotgun he clutched with two hands.

"Three men in each van," Rusty said as the crew split up into two different vans.

Pop could tell by the look on Rusty's face that it was about to go down like a plane crash.

"Yo, King, you ain't ready yet?" Bamboo yelled to the next room.

"Be there in a second," King responded. He stood in the next room strapping on his bulletproof vest and making sure his twin .45s were fully loaded.

"Damn, nigga, it took you long enough," Bamboo said, ready to take his wife out for her birthday. "You know we got reservations," he reminded the big man.

"Sorry about that, boss man," King apologized.

"Why don't you lay off him a little bit?" Nancy said, walking toward the front door.

"The rest of you mu'fuckas find something to do, just don't disrespect my house," Bamboo instructed as he, Nancy, and King headed out the front door.

Once in the all-black Denali with smoke-tinted windows,

King made the engine come to life and headed for the restaurant. As King drove toward the highway he noticed two mini-vans back-to-back speed past him. The bodyguard paused for a second then paid the mini-vans no mind, and continued toward the high way.

"Yo, me, Pop, and Pooh going through the front door, you three take the back door," Rusty ordered, screwing the silencers on his twin 9 mm's.

Once Pooh reached the front door, he aimed his shotgun at the door and shot it off the hinges. *Boom!*

Rusty was the first one in the house, followed by Pop. "Everybody on the fuckin' floor now!" Pop yelled, letting two shots off into the ceiling to let the men in the house know he meant business.

Seconds later, the three other gunmen came busting through the back door. Each man wore a ski mask making sure their identity was concealed. Once they had control of the situation, Rusty made sure he shot each man in the back of the head one by one execution-style.

"What we do now?" Pooh asked.

"We wait," Rusty answered quickly as he cut off all the lights in the house.

Bamboo and Nancy were enjoying their meal, while King stood up watching over the rest of the rich people eat their food, making sure no trouble came the couple's way.

"This shit is the bomb," Bamboo said, cutting off another piece of his steak and placing it in his mouth.

"Thanks, baby, for taking me to my favorite restaurant,"

Nancy said, sipping on her watermelon martini. "It's just sad that the only time we get to go out together is on my birthday." She pouted like a baby.

"Come on, babes, you know I will be busy a few more months and this shit is going to be all over with," Bamboo said with little energy.

"You always say that," she reminded him.

"Nah, I'm dead-ass this time. I was thinking about taking a year off. Just me and you to go enjoy ourselves on a nice island or something, what you think?" he asked her.

"Aw, my baby is the best," she said, feeling all good inside.

"I think I'm ready to go now baby," Nancy said, licking her lips. Once Bamboo saw what she had in mind it was a wrap; he could already feel his wife's warm mouth sliding up and down his dick. He knew exactly how freaky his wife could be, especially when she had a few drinks in her system, not to mention it was her birthday.

"Check, please," Bamboo said, flagging down the waiter, not wasting any time.

"Where the fuck is this clown?" Rusty said aloud as he peeked through the blinds. "This mu'fucka getting me tight, I'ma really hurt this nigga when he finally bring his ass home."

"He's going to have to come back home tonight, we've just got to be patient," Pop stated quietly as they continued to wait.

"Yo, King, keep your eyes on the road," Bamboo said, unzipping his zipper.

When Bamboo pulled out his love stick, Nancy was all over

him. She quickly made Bamboo's dick disappear like a magic trick as she placed the whole thing in her mouth.

"Damn," Bamboo moaned as he guided his wife's head up and down with his hand.

Twenty minutes later King pulled up in the driveway.

"Hold up, hold up, something ain't right. Why the fuck is all the lights out?" Bamboo asked, pulling out his Desert Eagle. "Let me call Danny real quick and see what's poppin'," he said as he pulled out his cell phone. "Something ain't right, Danny ain't answering his phone—back the fuck up out of here," Bamboo ordered, sensing something was wrong.

"What them fools doing out there?" Pop asked.

"They just sitting there in the driveway," Rusty answered as he heard a phone ringing. "Whose phone is that?" he asked, looking around.

"That's his phone," Pooh answered, pointing to the dead man sprawled out across the floor.

Seconds later, Rusty saw the Denali start to back out the driveway.

"Come on, they trying to leave!!" Rusty yelled as he ran to the door.

Once Rusty snatched open the front door, Pop aimed his Mac 10 at the Denali and pulled the trigger.

Pat, tat, tat, tat, tat!

Bamboo and Nancy quickly took cover as shattered glass showered their bodies.

"Get us the fuck out of here!" Bamboo yelled from the backseat, draping his body over Nancy's.

As King went to place the truck in drive, Rusty ran straight up to the front of the truck and let off five shots into the big man's chest. The impact from the shots caused King's body to jerk back and forth like he was having a seizure. Somehow the big man remained focused and stepped on the gas. Before Rusty could get out of the way, the Denali plowed into him, sending him flying on top of the hood. As King bent the corner, Rusty went flying out into the middle of the street. Before the Denali cleared the corner, Pop made sure he shot out the back window, hoping he might catch a head or two.

"Come on, we have to get out of here!" Pooh yelled, helping Rusty get back to his feet.

When King made it around the corner, he pulled over to avoid an accident. "I can't drive no more, I think my fuckin' ribs are broken," he cried out in pain as he peeled off his bulletfilled vest.

"Nancy get the fuck in the front seat," Bamboo ordered as he hopped out the Denali and helped King crawl into the backseat. Before Bamboo could get in the driver's seat three blue-and-white cop cars came to a screeching stop right in front of him.

"Keep your hands where I can see them," the officer yelled as he called for more backup on his walkie-talkie.

"Yo, call an ambulance—we got a man shot in the backseat," Bamboo said as he placed his hands behind his head and dropped down to his knees, already knowing the procedure.

"Miss, I'm going to need you to step out the vehicle as well," the officer said, aiming his weapon at the woman in the backseat.

"Hang in there, King," Nancy whispered as she kissed the big man on his forehead and got down on her knees next to her husband.

"Yo, grab his legs," Pop yelled as him and Pooh struggled to get Rusty in the back of the van. Once everyone was in the van, the van quickly burned rubber.

"You a'ight?" Pooh asked, looking down at Rusty.

"Yeah, I'm good," Rusty said, clearly in pain. "Did we get that nigga?"

"I don't know," Pop answered. "I doubt it, though."

"Mu'fucka knew we was in there." Rusty winced in pain. "That's why he ain't get out the car."

"How did he know?" Pooh asked.

"How the fuck would I know," Rusty huffed. "And slow this mu'fucka down before we get pulled over."

"You need to go to a hospital?" Pop asked.

"Fuck outta here," Rusty growled. "Only pussies go to the hospital if they ain't shot or stabbed."

"A'ight, fuck it, just stay in pain then," Pop said as the whole van erupted with laughter.

"Fuck that, just take me home," Rusty said, mad that the original mission wasn't accomplished.

"Don't even worry about it, we gon' get him next time," Pop said as each man rode in silence for the rest of the ride.

Chapter Nine

Fresh stood in his hospital room getting his things ready when he heard a light knock on his door. He quickly rushed to the door hoping it was Amanda. His whole mood changed when he saw the Chinese detective standing on the other side of the door with an evil smirk on his face.

"What the fuck do you want?" Fresh asked stiffly.

"I just want to ask you a few questions," the detective said, inviting himself inside the room. "A couple homicides went down last night. You wouldn't know anything about that, would you?"

"How the fuck would I know anything while I'm laying up in here?" Fresh asked, not even looking at the detective.

"You think if I showed you some pictures you could identify the man or men who shot you?"

"Nah, B. I don't know who did what, understand? Is that all? Because I'm not saying nothing else without my lawyer present," Fresh said coldly as he continued packing his bag.

"Well, here's my card. If you remember anything give me a call," the Chinese Detective said, handing Fresh his card.

"Yeah, right!" Fresh chuckled, tossing the card in the trash right in front of the detective. "I already told you. I don't know shit."

***

"What's good, my dude?" Pop asked as he bumped shoulders with the detective as he walked in the room.

The Chinese Detective didn't say a word; he just gave Pop and Fresh a cold stare.

"Fuck up out of here with that bullshit," Pop growled, matching the Chinese man's stare.

"We'll meet again," The Detective said, backing out of the room, never taking his eyes off of the two drug dealers.

"Yeah, I'll see you in hell, cocksucker!" Pop said, slamming the door shut behind the Detective. "I can't stand them mu'fuckas, B. always sniffing around and shit."

"It comes with the business," Fresh reminded the young soldier. "Where the fuck is Rusty?"

"He got injured on the job last night," Pop replied, looking at the floor.

"Word? How did it go last night?" Fresh asked.

"Fifty-fifty—we hit up his house and about five of his soldiers. Oh, and Rusty hit up the bodyguard something serious, but we didn't hit him, but the nigga got picked up by the cops though," Pop informed as he grabbed Fresh's bag for him.

"Rusty took a bullet?" Fresh asked.

"Nah, he got hit by a truck. He a'ight though, just got some bruised ribs and a few scrapes," Pop answered quickly.

"Damn, y'all niggas was getting it poppin' last night," Fresh chuckled as they headed to the parking lot. "This is only the beginning, because I ain't stopping until that mu'fucka ain't breathing no more, you dig?"

"You know I can dig it," Pop said, placing Fresh's bag in the trunk.

"Oh, shit, I see you doing big things while I was gone," Fresh said, admiring Pop's new car.

"You know I had to cop some wheels." Pop smiled as he

hopped in the driver's seat, stuck his key in the ignition, and started up the car.

"I'm proud of you, B. For real you a true, loyal soldier," Fresh said.

"You looking out for me, why wouldn't I do the same for you?" Pop asked, stopping at the red light.

"How would you like a promotion?" Fresh asked.

"Come on, or you kidding or what?" he answered, smiling from ear to ear.

"A'ight, this is what I'm going to do to show my appreciation. I got this new corner that I'm about to put work on and I want you to run it thorough, a'ight? I'm going to get workers for you and all that, you cool with that?"

"Yeah, I can handle that, that's a dream come true," Pop responded.

"Good, because it's about to be a few changes around here, plus, my man, Tito, will be coming home next week, so I guess I'll give him your old position," Fresh said as his face crumbled up from the pain.

"Yeah, I heard about Tito, I heard he's a real live wire," Pop said, making a right turn.

"Yeah, that nigga do be bugging sometimes," Fresh admitted. "You two should get along though."

"So what's your plans for tonight?" Pop asked, changing the subject.

"I'm going straight home. I have a lot of making up to do with Amanda. My other shorty sent me some flowers and shit, so you know she started flippin'."

"Damn, you slipping," Pop said as he pulled up right in front of Fresh's crib.

"Yo, I'm out, get with me tomorrow so we can set you up for this promotion, a'ight?" Fresh said, giving Pop a pound.

"A'ight, bet," he answered as he waited until Fresh disappeared inside his house before he pulled off.

Later on that night Pop sat on the bench smoking some piff, thinking about the promotion Fresh had given him. This was a big promotion—instead of being a goon now he would become a boss and have his own spot to run. Shit was funny like that in the hood, though, because last year Pop would have never thought that he would be running his own block. Everybody always told him that drugs were bad, but if it wasn't for drugs he would still have to stick people up just to get himself something to eat at night. Pop's thoughts were rudely interrupted when he noticed his little sister walking with her head down.

"Yo, come here!" Pop yelled, waving little Brittany over. "What's wrong with you?"

"Mommy stole some man's money, now he's upstairs beating her up," Brittany said as a tear escaped from the corner of her eye.

"Damn, that's fucked-up," Pop said aloud, feeling sorry for his little sister before changing the subject. "So what you been doing upstairs all day?" he asked quickly.

"Nothing, just watching TV but we don't even have no cable, no toys, no nothing," little Brittany said in a close-to-whining tone.

"A'ight, bet, this what I'm going to do. I'm going to buy you a Playstation 3, a'ight?" Pop said, ruffling his little sister's hair.

"You promise?" little Brittany asked excitedly with her eyes lighting up like a Christmas tree.

"Yeah, I promise I'm going to bring it to the house tomorrow afternoon. You just have to promise me you will cheer up, okay?" he told her.

"Oh, thank you so much, Pop," Brittany said as she gave her big brother a big hug, then skipped off to the playground.

"A little girl shouldn't have to live like that," Pop said to himself as he watched his little sister head to the playground. Pop's thoughts were quickly interrupted when he felt his Nextel vibrating.

"What's good, who this?" Pop asked with authority.

"Damn, how many girls you got calling you? It's Melissa," she said.

"Oh, what's good, ma?" he greeted.

"Nothing, you busy?" she asked.

"Nah, not at the moment. Why? What's goodie?" Pop said trying to sound extra-smooth.

"Nothing, I was just seeing if you wanted to come through for a little while and chill since I don't got school in the morning," she said.

"*Claro,*" Pop answered, letting her know that he would be there, using the only Spanish he knew, trying to impress her.

"Okay, I'm in apartment 11J," she said.

"Okay, cool, I'll be there in about twenty minutes," Pop replied, glancing down at his watch.

"Okay, *papi,*" Melissa replied, pressing the end button on her cordless.

"What the fuck took you so long to bail me out?" Bamboo growled as he shot Nancy and his lawyer a cold stare.

"Nigga, I been sitting in this mu'fucka for about eight hours so don't start no bullshit," Nancy spat, rolling her eyes.

"So, how shit looking?" Bamboo asked, looking at his lawyer.

"Well, basically, they don't got nothing on you, it's really

King that's fucked since he said the guns and vest were his. All you have to do is keep your nose clean and keep reporting back and forth to court until this shit blows over," the lawyer said confidently.

"That's what I'm talking about, that's why I pay you the big bucks," Bamboo said, snatching Nancy's pocketbook. "Yo, here, make sure you put money on King's books, and pick up his case," Bamboo ordered as he handed the lawyer an envelope full of money.

"Will do, Mr. Bamboo," the lawyer said, stuffing the envelope in his briefcase. "Y'all make sure y'all drive home safely, okay?"

"Yeah, you too," Bamboo said as he slid in the passenger seat of Nancy's car.

"This little nigga Fresh thinks he can play with the big boys, huh? I got something for that clown," Bamboo said out loud to nobody in particular.

Bamboo's only mission was to erase Fresh from the earth, and he planned on doing that by any means necessary.

"It's about time you got here," Melissa said, stepping to the side so Pop could enter.

"My fault—I had to go pick up some yak real quick," Pop slurred, already feeling saucy from the liquor he consumed earlier. Pop had to do a double-take when he noticed what Melissa was wearing.

She wore some red tight booty shorts with some red furry slippers along with a tight black wife beater. The ponytail that she wore made it easier for Pop to see all of her pretty features.

"I thought you had forgotten about me for a minute," Pop said, undressing Melissa with his eyes.

"How could I forget about you with your fine self?" Melissa

questioned, looking Pop dead in his eyes. "So, how's your family?" she asked, trying to change the subject.

"They cool," Pop answered quickly.

"How's your mother?"

"She's all right, I guess," Pop said, shrugging his shoulders.

"You guess?" Melissa asked.

"Yeah, me and my moms don't get along too well," Pop answered.

"What about your father?" she moved on to the next question.

"I don't know him!" Pop replied stiffly.

"You don't know your father?" Melissa asked in disbelief.

"He went out for a snack one day and never came back," Pop answered, finishing off his cup, only to fill it right back to the top.

"Did he get killed?" Melissa asked weakly.

"Nah, he just never came back," Pop said in a flat tone.

"Aw, poor baby, come here," Melissa said, placing Pop's face on her firm but soft breast. "Did you hear from Fresh since he got out the hospital?"

"Yeah, I picked him up from the hospital," Pop answered.

"Him and my sister is crazy, they always fighting and shit," Melissa laughed before she continued. "That nigga Fresh bought her a new car and he know she can't drive."

"Word? What kind of car did he get her?" Pop asked.

"He got her an '06 Intrepid," Melissa answered quickly.

"Damn, he must have really fucked-up bad this time," Pop chuckled.

When Melissa got up to pour herself another drink, she started feeling the effects of the Grey Goose. Instantly, her mind went back to the other day when she was in Pop's whip and how he had made her body feel.

"Fuck that I'm about to make a move," Melissa said under

her breath as she quickly downed her drink, and made her way back over to the couch where Pop sat.

"I need to ask you a question," Melissa slurred as she hopped up on top of Pop, straddling her legs on each side of him.

"Ask me whatever you want," he said as his dick got harder than Chinese arithmetic.

"Pop, what exactly are you looking for?" she asked, looking him dead in his eyes.

"I don't understand," Pop said, leaning back further on the couch.

"Are you looking for a girlfriend, or do you just want to fuck me every now and then?" Melissa asked, not beating around the bush.

"I'm looking for a real woman that's willing to hold her man down when she have to," Pop answered.

"Pop, don't bullshit me, I haven't had a man in over a year and a half, I'm looking for something that's going to be real. All the men I dealt with in my past all did me dirty, so if you just want to fuck then I'm going to have to ask you to leave," she said, hoping and praying Pop would be different.

"Come on, baby, you know I wouldn't do that to you," Pop lied. Little did Melissa know but Pop had been feeling her for the longest.

"Pop, I don't want to sound crazy, but if you break my heart I'm going to kill you," Melissa said seriously.

"Come on, ma, why you trying to disrespect me like that?" Pop asked.

"I'm sorry, Pop, I just don't want to get hurt again," Melissa said as she gripped Pop's chin and planted a big wet kiss on his lips.

"Baby, why would I want to hurt you?" Pop asked as he lifted up Melissa's wife beater, exposing her pretty round breasts.

"Pop, if you keep it real with me I'll keep it real with you," Melissa whispered as she slowly took off her wife beater and tossed it on the floor. She kissed him one more time as she noticed his empty cup. "Papi, let me get you a refill," she said as she stood up and slid out of her booty shorts, then headed to the kitchen.

Melissa's ass was so fat that her butt cheeks swallowed the red thong she wore. All that could be seen as she walked to the kitchen was her ass jiggling all over the place. The top of her red thong, the G-string could no longer be seen.

Pop couldn't believe what was about to go down. As he sat waiting for Melissa to return, he felt his Nextel vibrating. He looked at the caller ID and saw that it was Nika who was calling. Without even thinking twice, he turned off his cell phone. He knew he was wrong but at the moment the alcohol was in control and the emotions he was feeling for Melissa were too strong to deny.

"Bring that donkey ass over here," Pop slurred as Melissa made her way back over to the couch.

"What you still doing fully dressed?" she asked, placing one hand on her hip. "You ain't getting this drink until you naked," she warned.

Without hesitation Pop did as he was told. Once he was naked, Melissa handed him his drink and turned on some music.

Once the music started flowing Melissa decided to put on a show for her guest and started shaking her ass.

Pop pulled out a few singles and playfully tossed them on the floor as he continued to watch the show. He was surprised when he saw Melissa break down into a split; because of how thick she was he couldn't picture her doing it. Not only did she drop down into a split, but she bounced twice, then came back up effortlessly.

"Fuck this bullshit," Pop said as he stood up, hard dick and all. "Yo, bring that ass over here."

Once he got his hands on Melissa he aggressively ripped off her thong and tossed her on the couch.

"Just tell me how you want it, papi, however you want it it's yours," Melissa moaned, already anticipating how good the dick was going to feel. "It's been a long time so take it easy," she begged as she got on all fours on the couch.

"I got you, ma," Pop replied smoothly as he rolled on a condom.

Melissa's pussy was so wet from anticipation that Pop just slid right in with no problem.

"Easy, *papi*," Melissa moaned, pleased at the size of Pop.

He slowly eased his way inside, making sure he was fully in before he started to pick up the pace. He couldn't believe how warm, tight, and wet Melissa's pussy was.

"Mmmm . . ." Melissa moaned as she wrapped her legs around Pop's waist and began to claw at his back. Pop then took Melissa's legs and placed them all the way back to her shoulders, as he proceeded to get deeper and deeper inside Melissa's pussy. He watched as his dick disappeared then reappeared in and out of Melissa's pussy. Once Pop was sure Melissa was broken in he quickly turned her around on all fours and began fuckin' the shit out of her. With each stroke delivered, Melissa's ass cheeks jiggled all over the place as she began throwing her ass back with force. Pop tried to look away and not look at Melissa's ass jiggling in his face so he could last a little longer, but that trick didn't work this time. He quickly pulled out and came all over Melissa's butt.

"Well, damn," Pop said, smiling and breathing heavily. "I ain't know it was like that."

"Whatever, you just better not ever take me or this pussy for granted," Melissa said, smirking as she walked to the bathroom. Pop just watched Melissa's ass cheeks, which still had fresh cum on them, continue to jiggle as she disappeared inside the bathroom.

Chapter Ten

"Did you get the flowers and balloons I sent you?" Vanessa asked as she was giving Fresh an oil massage.

"Yeah, I got them and I got into a big-ass fight over them too," Fresh responded as he gave her a slight grin.

"Shit, she lucky I was out of town, because we would have both just been fighting. I would have been at the hospital and you know it," Vanessa said confidently.

"Yeah, I know," Fresh said, happy that she was out of town on business. "Yo, I'm going to have come back and see you tomorrow, okay?" he said as he stood up to leave.

"Okay, baby, that's cool," Vanessa responded as she watched Fresh put on his jacket as he stood up to leave.

"Be careful out there in that rain, and make sure you drive safely," she warned.

"I got you, baby," Fresh stated as he stepped outside and quickly ran to his car door so he wouldn't get too wet.

Vanessa stood in the doorway until Fresh's taillights disappeared in the darkness before she went back inside. Fresh didn't even get one foot in the door before Amanda was already bitching. "Where the fuck you been all day?" she asked, snaking her neck, looking at the clock.

"Outside!" Fresh answered quickly, not in the mood for an argument.

"Where at outside?" she asked, looking for trouble.

"Yo, don't be questioning me. I was taking care of some business," Fresh snarled in a nasty tone.

"I'm your wife—I have the right to know where you are at all times," Amanda fumed.

"Wife?" Fresh said, letting out a soft laugh. "I don't have time for this shit. I'm going to take a shower."

"Why you rushing to take a shower? You haven't even been home for five minutes," she asked with bad intentions. Fresh didn't answer; instead he just went straight in the bathroom and closed the door.

"This mu'fucka got a lot of nerve cheating on me as good as I am to him," Amanda said to herself as she heard the shower turn on. Once Amanda was sure that Fresh was in the shower, she went in the bedroom and started snooping around. The first thing she picked up was Fresh's sidekick. As soon as she picked it up the sound of it ringing startled her, catching her off guard and causing it to fumble around in her hands. Once she regained control she looked at the device that read NEW MESSAGE. It was from Vanessa.

Hey, baby, I'm just checking to see if you made it home safe, and out of the rain, well hit me back later 'cause I'm about to take a nap, you know that dick always put me to sleep LOL . . . I'm out, later.

After Amanda read that message, rage and anger could be seen all in her face. She immediately headed straight to the bathroom.

"I thought you didn't know any fuckin' Vanessa?" Amanda yelled, snatching back the shower curtain.

"What the fuck are you talking about?" Fresh asked, not sure what was going on or what to say.

"This what the fuck I'm talking about!" Amanda growled, showing Fresh the message from Vanessa in his sidekick.

Fuck, I'm slipping yo, Fresh thought as he tried to not look surprised.

"Bitch, what the fuck is you doing going through my shit?" Fresh yelled as he back-slapped Amanda with his wet hand.

"Fuck you, mu'fucka! You going to get what's coming to you," she promised as she tossed Fresh's sidekick in the toilet, then headed to the bedroom.

This bitch is fuckin' crazy, Fresh thought as he hopped straight out of the shower and headed to the bedroom, dripping wet. "What the fuck are you doing?"

Amanda didn't respond; instead, she just continued to pack her duffel bag and grab the rest of her belongings. "I hope it was worth it, you heartless bastard," she snarled as she grabbed her keys off the dresser. She headed outside in the pouring rain, heated out of her mind. When Amanda got outside she found out that the storm had gotten much worse, but she didn't care. She just headed outside, threw her shit in the trunk, and hopped in the driver's seat of her Intrepid.

"Baby, come back inside so we can talk about this," Fresh yelled from the doorway as he partially stepped out, but it was no use as he watched his woman pull out into the storm.

"I shouldn't have left," Amanda said out loud, crying her eyes out, trying to stay focused on the road. It was raining so hard that she could barely see a thing. Her ringing cell phone didn't help the matter—it just made it worst.

"Stop fuckin' calling me!" Amanda yelled out loud, looking at the cell phone as if it was going to talk back.

After ten minutes of nonstop ringing she couldn't take it any more. "What the fuck do you want?" she yelled into her cell phone as she lost control of the vehicle. Before she could regain control of the vehicle she saw a woman and a child in front of her headlights. Immediately, she stomped her brakes. The back tires slid, causing the vehicle to swerve. Before Amanda knew it the young child bounced off her windshield and up into the air. Amanda bumped her head on the steering wheel as the vehicle came to a complete stop. Blood trickled from her forehead as she stepped out of the vehicle.

"What the fuck did you do?" the woman screamed out, clutching her dead daughter's head in her arms. "You didn't see that red light?" the woman asked, her face full of tears.

"No, I didn't see a red light," Amanda mumbled, feeling sorry for the woman standing in front of her. All she could do was say sorry. Amanda was shaking nervously as she put a hand over her mouth in disbelief.

"Yeah, you going to be sorry," the woman snarled as she dialed 911 in her cell phone. Not knowing what to do, Amanda quickly hopped back in her car and fled the scene.

"Hey, get back here, you murderer," the woman yelled as tears streamed down her face and she watched the car that killed her daughter disappear into the night.

"What the fuck did I just do?" Amanda asked herself out loud as she tried to watch the road through her cracked windshield. "All I have to do is get to Melissa's house so I can ditch this car, and I'll be all right," she told herself over and over again. Right before Amanda approached the highway she saw flashing lights in her rearview mirror. "Oh my God, I'm going to jail," she said repeatedly to herself as she pulled over and from her rearview mirror watched the white police officer make his way to her vehicle.

"Miss, can you please step out of the vehicle?" the red-faced officer asked, shining his bright flashlight in Amanda's face. Once out of the vehicle the red-faced officer roughly pushed her on the hood of the wet car and proceeded to search her just as rough. "Miss, put your hands behind your back," he said in a smooth tone as he handcuffed her, then placed her in the backseat of his squad car. "I hope you got a good lawyer," the officer chuckled as he slammed the back door to the squad car.

Chapter Eleven

"Wow, look at how real these people look!" little Brittany bragged as she and her other brother played the new game that Pop had just bought them. They were sitting, having a good time—that was, until Teresa came stumbling in. "What the fuck is that y'all in here playing?" Teresa slurred, with her eyes bloodshot red.

"PlayStation 3," little Brittany answered proudly.

"Where the fuck did y'all get that from?"

"Pop brought it for us," Brittany answered again.

"Pop brought it for y'all?" Teresa asked skeptically. She looked at the game as she swayed back and forth, trying to keep her balance.

"Didn't I tell you he's not allowed in my house anymore?" she barked, snatching the plug out of the wall. "I'm taking this mu'fucka to the pawnshop," she said loudly as she placed the system in a garbage bag, and headed back toward the door. The sighs of the kids and sounds of them smacking their lips in disappointment filled the air as they looked at Teresa drunkenly gathering the cords.

"We can't never have nothing nice," Little Brittany mumbled under her breath in disappointment.

"I heard that, you little bitch," Teresa said as she bent down and slapped the little girl across her face with all of her might. "You get that disrespectful shit from that idiot Pop," she yelled as she headed out the door with the PS3.

**

"What the fuck you mean you in jail?" Fresh yelled angrily into the receiver.

"Mu'fucka, what part don't you understand? It's your fault why I'm in here anyway," Amanda barked back.

"Who the fuck you talking to like that?" Fresh questioned.

"Fresh, don't play with me," she warned.

"What you mean don't play with you?" Fresh asked as he looked at the receiver to make sure he wasn't bugging.

"All I know is that I better get bailed out before the night is out or else! As much shit as you done put me through, shit," Amanda stated boldly.

"You'll be out before the night is out," Fresh said as he slammed the phone down in her ear.

"Yo, you ready to go pick this nigga Tito up?" Rusty asked quietly, sensing something was wrong.

"Huh," Fresh asked, snapping out of his inner thoughts.

"You ready to pick up Tito?" Rusty asked again.

"Yeah, let's be out," Fresh answered as him and Rusty headed out the door and hopped in the Range Rover.

"Yo, you know that nigga Bernard?" Rusty asked as he pulled out into traffic.

"You talking about that nigga you took with you on the Bamboo hit?" Fresh asked, searching his memory.

"Yeah, that nigga," Rusty began excitedly. "My man told me he just got picked up the other day by them five-oh."

"You think he talking?" Fresh asked quickly.

Rusty shrugged his shoulders. "I don't know, he ain't really a street nigga like that. I just used him that night 'cause I needed one more man so it probably won't be too hard to get to roll over."

"Do what you gotta do," Fresh said without thinking twice

about it. His motto was if you had to think about whether a person would snitch or not, then more than likely he would turn out to be a problem, and the last thing Fresh needed was another problem.

"You heard that nigga Tito getting out today, right?" Pooh asked, spitting out some sunflower seeds.

"Yeah, I heard it's supposed to be a big party for him tonight," Pop replied quickly.

"I heard it's going to be mad hoes there and all that," Pooh said excitedly.

"We'll see," Pop said as he noticed little Brittany walking with her head down again.

"I'll be right back," Pop said, making his way over to his little sister.

"Yo, what's wrong with you?" Pop asked.

"Mommy took the game and pawned it," little Brittany said, feeling ashamed of her mother.

"Brittany, please tell me you lying," Pop asked seriously.

"Nope, she took it to the pawnshop earlier," Brittany tattled.

"Damn, you know how much I paid for that shit," Pop growled.

"The people looked so real on that game too," little Brittany added.

"Is Mommy upstairs right now?" Pop asked heatedly.

"Yeah, she just woke up," Brittany answered.

"Okay, I want you to go to the park and play, all right?"

"Okay, Pop," little Brittany said as she headed to the park.

"This bitch must be crazy," Pop said to himself as he went to go pay Ms. Teresa a little visit.

***

"Damn, it feels good to be home," Tito said, giving Rusty and Fresh a pound followed by a hug.

"Glad to have you back home," Fresh said, handing Tito a brown paper bag full of money.

"Good looking, baby, It's going to be just like old times out here, B," Tito stated, happy to be home.

"You know I had to bring your baby girl," Rusty cut in, placing a P89 in Tito's hand. Tito looked at the gun and let out a slight chuckle. "Damn it feels good to get away from those crackers and those fuckin' mountains," he said as he took a brief pause, admiring his P89 Ruger. "I'm home now, baby, you already know what time it is," Tito said as the Range Rover pulled off, headed to the big city.

When Pop entered his mother's small apartment it was junky and dirty as usual. He stepped over the clothes and random trash as he made his way over to Teresa, who was sitting on the couch slouching.

"What the fuck you doing in my mu'fuckin' house?" Teresa asked, frowning at the sight of her son.

"Yo, where the fuck is my money?" Pop asked bluntly, as he ignored the several roaches on the wall playing follow the leader.

"What money you talking about?" Teresa asked, dumbfounded.

"Bitch, stop playing stupid with me. You know what money I'm talking about," Pop said, kicking over a bag of dirty clothes that stood in front of him.

"Boy, you must have lost your fuckin' mind!" Teresa yelled as she hopped up and back-slapped Pop dead across his face. The impact from the blow busted his lip and caused his hat to fly off. Instantly Pop turned and caught his moms with a right hook followed by a sharp uppercut, sending Teresa crashing into the kitchen table. He snapped.

"That's just what I wanted you to do, you dumb mu'fucka. Now you going straight to jail," Teresa snarled through a pair of bloody lips as she held her jaw. Pop quickly ran out of the house when he saw his mother reaching for the phone and disappeared into the staircase. Once outside Pop made his way straight to Nika's house, so he could hide out until it was time to go to the party. When Pop stepped in the crib Nika was naked placing lotion on her sexy body.

"Hey, baby, what you doing home so early?" Nika asked, happy her man was home.

"I just had to fuck my moms up!" Pop blurted out.

"Please tell me you lying," Nika said, walking around naked.

"I had just bought my little sister a PS3, and my mother pawned it the next day."

"So you going to risk going to jail over six hundred dollars?" Nika asked, not understanding the point.

"It's not about the money, it's about the principle, you dig?" Pop replied.

"I hear what you saying, but you still have to be smarter than that, because you know your mother will call the cops on you in a New York minute," Nika reminded him.

"Yeah, you right. I'm going to go take a shower real quick; hopefully, that will make me feel better," Pop said as he removed his shirt.

"Pop, is it all right if I go to the club tonight with a few of my friends?" Nika asked as she began to paint her toenails.

"I don't care," he answered. "I'm going too but I really don't want to!" he said as he closed the bathroom door. While Pop was in the shower, Nika came in the bathroom and sat on the toilet seat, hoping to cheer him up.

"Baby, no matter what happens you know I'm going to be right here by your side the whole way," Nika promised him.

"I know, baby," Pop responded as he cut off the water and hopped out of the shower. That last comment made him love Nika even more—knowing she had his back 100 percent was all he needed to hear. Once fully dressed, he pulled out his cell phone and dialed Pooh's number.

"Yo, where you at?" Pop asked.

"Nigga, I'm downstairs waiting for you," Pooh answered excitedly.

"Cool. I'm coming down right now," Pop said, ending the conversation.

"Baby, I'm out. I'll see you at the club, okay?" Pop yelled over his shoulder.

"Okay, boo, be careful," Nika said as she continued cleaning up the house. As Pop headed down the steps he felt bad about lying to Nika, but the truth was he loved her and Melissa, no way he would be able to choose.

"Yo, the cops are out here looking for you," Pooh said as he gave his friend a pound.

"Word? Where them clowns at right now?" Pop asked, looking over both shoulders.

"I don't know, they were out here with your moms earlier," Pooh said as he slid in the passenger side of the Magnum.

"Those mu'fuckas going to have to catch me, you dig?" Pop said, pulling out of his parking spot.

"You about to finally meet Tito," Pooh said, letting out a light chuckle.

"What's so funny?"

"You'll see when you meet him," Pooh answered.

"Yeah, a'ight," Pop said, turning up the volume on his Lil Wayne CD.

When Pop pulled up in front of Fresh's warehouse, cars were parked everywhere—you would have thought the president had just got out of jail. "Yo, pass me my ratchet from out of the glove compartment," Pop said, sticking the 9 mm in his waistband.

As soon as Pop stepped foot inside the warehouse he spotted Tito immediately. They way the man handled himself demanded attention. Tito was a fast-talking Dominican who didn't take no shit from nobody, and was known for being very disrespectful.

"Let me introduce you to my main man, Pop," Fresh stated plainly as him and Tito walked over to where Pop and Pooh stood.

"So, this suppose to be my new replacement, huh?" Tito asked, laughing loudly, making a scene. "This baby-faced cocksucker wouldn't hurt a fuckin' fly," Tito said cockily, not caring about the man standing in front of him. Little did he know, he was talking to a killer.

"Who the fuck is you talking to like that, B?" Pop asked, ready to get it on and poppin'.

"Make your move, chump," Tito growled, getting all up in Pop's face.

"Y'all niggas chill the fuck out. We all on the same team," Fresh said, stepping in between the two men.

"I'm home now, B. Get use to me being around, my dude," Tito said, looking Pop up and down like he was a child.

"You all talk, but no action," Pop shot back calmly and not backing down.

"Yo, I said that's enough, we all on the same fuckin' team." Fresh paused before he continued. "We all going to the club tonight to have a good time. I don't want to hear no more shit out of you two," he warned.

"Yo, Fresh, I'm just going to meet you at the club, I'm about to head that way now," Pop said, walking out of the warehouse.

Once Pop was gone Tito started up again. "Yo, Fresh, why you fuckin' with these young chumps? He ain't no soldier."

"Don't judge a book by its cover—that kid is more of a soldier then you think," Fresh assured him.

"Yeah, Pop ain't no punk. He be getting it in," Rusty added.

"Well, I ain't convinced," Tito responded, being the stubborn bull that he was. "He's going to have to make a believer out of me because honestly I don't see it in him." Tito busted out laughing as he poured himself another drink. In all reality he was jealous of Pop; he hated that a younger hustler had taken his spot while he was away. Tito didn't know how but he planned on getting his position back one way or another.

"I should of popped that nigga," Pop said out loud. "I knew he was going to throw on the fake tough-guy routine," he said as he felt his Nextel vibrating. When he looked at his caller ID he saw that it was Fresh.

"What's good?" Pop asked very uninterested.

"You a'ight, my nigga?" Fresh asked.

"Yeah, I'm good," Pop answered quickly.

"Don't worry about Tito. He's just happy to be home and a little overexcited," Fresh said, explaining his man's behavior.

"I see, but Fresh, you know I don't be with all that talking shit. Make sure you let that fool know that before I have to lay my hands on that boy," Pop said harshly.

"I got you, baby. I'm going to take care of it. We 'bout to head to the club now," Fresh said, hearing the anger in Pop's voice.

"A'ight, I'll see y'all inside," Pop said, closing his Nextel.

For the rest of the ride, all Pop could do was think about Tito. He hated the fact that he couldn't put his hands on the Dominican. He felt as if Tito was challenging him and Pop just couldn't see himself bowing down; something inside of him just wouldn't let him. As Pop pulled up in front of the club, he noticed it was hundreds of people crowded around the front as usual. He was about to place his 9 mm in the glove compartment, but his instinct told him to keep it on his waist.

"Where the fuck is Fresh at?" Amanda asked, ready to kill him.

"He's at the club, he sent Rusty to give me the money to bail you out," Melissa stated plainly.

"This mu'fucka got a lot of fuckin' nerves," Amanda said, trying to hold in her tears. "Take me to the fuckin' club, I need to talk to this mu'fucka," she demanded from the passenger side of the car.

When Pop stepped inside the club, it was jumping from wall to wall as usual. He headed straight for the bar, so he could get his mind right and scope out who was in the club. "Yo, let me get a bottle of Grey Goose," he yelled over the blasting music to the cute bartender. After a little flirting Pop headed straight toward the VIP section with his bottle in hand so he could sit down and just chill for a minute.

Ten minutes later, Fresh, Tito, Rusty, and the rest of the crew came strolling over to the VIP section. Pop paid them no mind as he focused on Nika and her girlfriend entering the club.

Nika wore a tight-fitting red skirt along with her red hooker boots that came up to her knees. As good as Nika looked, Pop knew what his plans were when they got back home.

Instantly, his heart dropped into his stomach when he saw Melissa and Amanda headed toward the VIP section. "What the fuck are they doing here?" Pop wondered. "I hope Melissa and Nika don't bump into each other," he said to himself, looking a little nervous.

"So you just going to leave a bitch for dead like that?" Amanda snarled, getting all up in Fresh's face.

"Why don't you go home and get you some rest," Fresh shot back, turning his back to her.

"Don't you turn your back on me, mu'fucka," Amanda yelled as she grabbed Fresh's wrist and spun him back around.

"Listen, bitch, nobody told you to run out the fuckin' house in a thunderstorm," Fresh said strongly.

"Fuck you, you heartless bastard," she growled as she grabbed a drink from off the table and tossed it in Fresh's face.

Rusty immediately grabbed Amanda and began to escort her out of the club. He didn't want to hurt Amanda because she was like family, but his job was to protect Fresh, and that's what he was going to do.

"You gonna get yours, mu'fucka!" Amanda yelled over her shoulder as she, Melissa, and Rusty disappeared into the crowd.

"Them Spanish bitches is crazy," Fresh said, feeling embarrassed as he dried himself off with a napkin, feeling like a sucker. Pop continued to mind his business as he got drunk by himself. The whole club went crazy when 50 Cent's new song came blaring through the speakers.

Pop stood over on the couch with his head down while the liquor took its effect. When Pop looked up he saw Tito all up in Nika's face. At first he thought the liquor was fuckin' with his mind, but as he did a double-take he realized he wasn't bugging.

"What's good, baby, what's your name?" Tito slurred, smelling like liquor.

"I don't have a name!" Nika responded, uninterested.

"Ma, stop stunting you know you feeling the God," Tito said, grabbing Nika's hand.

"Get ya fuckin' hands off of me, my man!" Nika said, jerking her hand away. "Beat it, you bum-ass nigga," she said as she and her girlfriend busted out laughing.

"Bitch, you ain't shit but a fuckin' gold digger anyway, but I'll tell you what you can do, you can kiss my ass with your tongue, you fuckin' slut!" Tito capped back, ready to slap both of the women without thinking twice.

"Yo, what's good? Is there a problem over here?" Pop asked, showing up right on time.

"Yeah, this thirsty bum-ass nigga is harassing me," Nika said, pointing at Tito.

"Harassing you?" Tito echoed, looking at Nika like she was insane. "Ma, you can't be serious. My worst slide look better than you on her worst day."

"Yo, this my shorty right here, so back off, a'ight?" Pop said, looking Tito dead in his eyes.

"Nigga, ain't nobody trying to talk to your little dirty-ass bitch," Tito said, not even thinking about backing down. "You need to step your bitch game up, my geez "cause this right here," he said pointing at Nika, "this is not a good look!" Tito said as he burst out laughing.

It took everything inside Pop to control his temper and not pistol-whip the Dominican. Tito saw the look on Pop's face and reacted.

"What's good? You wanna get it poppin'?" the Dominican said, always ready for action.

"Come on let's go," Nika said as she pulled Pop by his wrist, leading him out the club before things got out of hand.

"That's right, you better leave, mu'fucka!" Tito yelled. "And take that wack-ass bitch with you."

Pop checked the magazine on his 9 mm as soon as he stepped outside.

"I'm going to pop that nigga when he comes outside."

"He's not even worth it," Nika said, taking the gun and placing it in her purse. "You got way more to lose than that clown," she added, trying to calm Pop down.

"Yo, let's be out," Pop said as he noticed an unmarked car cruising slowly in their direction.

"Excuse me," a voice from inside the car yelled.

When Pop looked he couldn't believe who it was. The Chinese detective hopped out the unmarked car with his gun already drawn.

"Let me see those hands, buddy," he warned.

"We didn't even do nothing," Nika said, rolling her eyes at the Chinese man.

"Put your hands behind your back," the detective said aiming his .357 at Pop's chest.

"Chill out, Jet Li," Pop said, doing as he was told. Once the Detective handcuffed Pop, he thoroughly searched him, upset that he didn't find a weapon. He roughly threw him up against the unmarked car before he tossed him in the backseat.

"What's the charge? 'cause this is bullshit," Nika said rudely.

"Ma'am, your boyfriend assaulted his own mother earlier—now back off before I take you in with him," the man said seriously.

Nika quickly remembered the 9 mm that she had in her purse and passed her purse to her girlfriend, who was just standing around being a witness.

"All you cops are dirty, always fuckin' with black people, you Chinese mu'fucka," Nika spat as she watched the Chinese detective drive away with her man. As soon as the unmarked car was out of eyesight, Nika quickly ran to the corner and flagged down a cab so she could go home and get some money to bail her man out.

"So beating up on women must make you feel like a real tough guy, huh?" the Chinese detective asked, looking at Pop through his rearview mirror. Pop sucked his teeth at the Chinese man and continued to look out the window. He knew he would be out in a couple of hours, if that.

"Shut the fuck up and just drive," Pop huffed, shaking his head.

"The truth hurts, doesn't it?" The Chinese detective laughed, still looking at Pop through the rearview mirror.

"What the fuck you keep looking at?" Pop growled as he slid down and began kicking the fence in the detective's car. The Chinese detective quickly pulled the car over to the side of the road.

"You think you tough guy, huh?" The Chinese detective chuckled as he removed his night stick from underneath his seat and slid out the vehicle. He quickly walked to the back of the car and snatched open the back.

"Yo, what you doing?" Pop yelled in a panic as he began kicking his feet to keep the detective off of him. The Chinese detective caught Pop's leg as he was trying to kick and violently snatched him out the backseat of the car onto the concrete.

"Didn't I tell you to stop fuckin' with me?" the Chinese detective scolded as he beat Pop with the night stick like he was an animal.

"Fuckin' animal," the Chinese detective yelled as he roughly tossed Pop back in the car. "I can't stand you stupid-ass thugs," he huffed as got back in the driver's seat and continued on to the station.

"Yo, come with me outside for a second, I feel like I'm about to throw up," Rusty said, leaning on Bernard's shoulder for support.

"Damn, you that fucked-up?" Bernard laughed as he help escort Rusty through the club toward the exit.

Fresh watched Rusty and Bernard exit the club and all he could do was shake his head. He liked Bernard but he didn't like him enough to sit in a jail cell for the rest of his life.

"Oh, well," Fresh said out loud as he noticed Tito coming his way with a frown on his face. "What's wrong now?" Fresh asked, draping his arm around Tito.

"I don't like Pop," Tito huffed. "He ain't built for this business and I think you should let me take him out."

Fresh chuckled lightly. "Chill, Pop is good money. Trust me, once y'all get to know each other y'all going to get along fine."

"Nah, fuck all that chill shit," Tito huffed, waving Fresh off. "I got a gut feeling and you know my gut is never wrong."

"Listen, Tito, you just came home. Just chill out for a minute, you still on your jail shit. You home now, my nigga, leave that jail mentality shit in jail 'cause out here I'm gonna need you clear-minded," Fresh told him.

"Nah, I'm just saying—"

"Fuck what you saying," Fresh said, cutting Tito off. "Y'all my two best soldiers and I can't have y'all out here beefing and shit, so just chill the fuck out, if it's that serious you two just stay away from one another unless it's business, you dig?"

"Yeah, I hear you," Tito said, still feeling a little salty about the situation, but he played it cool because everything Fresh was saying was right.

"Remember, we do this to make money, we don't do this for bragging rights," Fresh said, refilling his glass along with Tito's

"Damn, I feel like shit," Rusty said hunched over by the curb still faking like he was sick. When he saw Bernard pull out his cell phone to make a call, he slowly removed a .380 from his waistband.

"Yo, nigga, come here real quick," Rusty said pretending like he was out of breath. Once Bernard was close enough Rusty quickly raised the .380 and let off two shots. One landed in Bernard's neck while the other bullet found a home in the upper part of his chest. Rusty watched Bernard's body hit the ground; the man's boot shook twice then he died. Rusty looked over both shoulders before stepping over the body and headed back inside the club.

After the club, Fresh hopped in his Lexus and turned up his music. He grabbed the blunt from out of his ashtray and lit it as he pulled out of his parking spot. "This chick better be awake," Fresh said to himself as he exited off the highway. Twenty minutes, later Fresh pulled into the empty parking spot. He stepped out his Lexus, feeling nice from the yak he had consumed earlier. As soon as Fresh's foot touched the curb, he heard the clicking sound of a gun, and felt cold stainless steel on the back of his head.

"You already know what this is, fam," the gunman said

in a deep voice. His identity was hidden by a hoodie and a bandana tied around his face.

"Chill, fam, let me talk to you for a second," Fresh said, attempting to turn around.

"Don't do it to yourself, playboy," the gunman said, pressing the burner deeper into the back of Fresh's head. "Fuck a talk," he said as he held the gun to the back of Fresh's head with one hand and searched through his pockets with the other hand.

"You know I'm going to see you again, right?" Fresh said with a smile.

"Yeah, well, next time bring a gun so at least you can have a chance," the gunman said as he hit Fresh in the back of his head with the gun knocking him out cold. Once the gunman saw that Fresh was knocked out he unlocked his Lexus, hopped in it, and pulled off leaving the hustler laid out in the middle of the street.

Three minutes later, Fresh woke up on the ground. "What the fuck," he whispered, holding the back of his head. He sat up and slowly looked around and saw a mini-crowd. Fresh quickly stood up and walked over to the first girl he saw. "You saw anything?" he asked.

"I just saw a man wearing a hoodie hit you in the back of your head with something, then drive off in your car," the woman answered honestly.

"You couldn't recognize who it was?" Fresh asked, still holding the back of his head.

"Nah, his face was all covered up," the lady told him.

Vanessa stepped out of her building and saw a mini-crowd standing around Fresh. Immediately her heart sank as she jogged over to where Fresh stood. "Baby, are you okay, what happened?" She asked in a fast paced voice.

"I just got robbed," Fresh said.

"Oh my God, are you okay, do you need me to take you to the hospital?"

"Nah, I'm good," Fresh answered. "Mu'fucka snuck me from behind," he said. Vanessa helped him to the building.

"You know I'm going to catch that fool, right?" Fresh said, refusing to let the situation die.

"I know you are, baby," Vanessa replied, knowing that Fresh wouldn't rest until he caught the person who had done this to him.

Chapter Twelve

Pop sat in his crib watching *BET* when he heard his phone ringing.

"What up?" Pop said into his cell phone.

"I need to see you," Fresh said before hanging up the phone.

Pop walked up in the warehouse and his attitude immediately changed when he saw Tito. From the look on Tito's face, Pop could tell that he was drunk.

"Glad you could make it," Fresh said as he passed the blunt to Rusty. "Yo, I need Tito, Pooh, and you to handle something for me."

Pop didn't really want to work with Tito, but he had to do what he had to do.

"What we gotta do?" Pop asked.

"It's this new guy in town," Fresh paused so he could inhale the weed smoke. "He calls himself setting up shop on a few of my corners. Word on the street is he holding mad bricks . . . I want those bricks and I need y'all to get them for me."

"Don't you even worry. Shit, I'ma make sure I personally teach this fuckin' cocksucker a lesson," Tito said, pounding on his chest. "You already know how I do," he said loudly as he gave Rusty a pound.

Pop sighed loudly as he just shook his head.

"You got a problem over there, fam?" Tito asked, turning his gaze on Pop.

"No problem over here," Pop said, throwing his hands up in surrender.

"That's what the fuck I thought," Tito countered.

"Y'all two niggas better chill the fuck out," Fresh said. "All this money out here and y'all wanna be arguing like some bitches." He paused. "Now this nigga bitch goes and gets her nails done every week at this place right here," Fresh said, handing Tito a piece of paper with the address on it along with a photo of the woman. "Get to her and she'll lead y'all straight to him."

"Say no more," Tito said, stuffing the photo and piece of paper down in his back pocket. "Come on, let's be out," he said as he exited the warehouse.

Pop knew he had to control his temper while out with Tito, knowing how ignorant and foolish the man could act. Pop slid in the passenger seat of Tito's gray Range Rover while Pooh climbed in the back.

"Yo, fam, don't be slamming my fuckin' door like that, B," Tito complained. "Once you get you Range Rover then that's when you can start slamming doors, until then don't be slamming my shit," Tito huffed as he looked for a CD. "Next time I'ma just smack the shit out you 'cause I'm tired of talking to you."

"Come on that shit ain't even that serious," Pooh said from the backseat, trying to defuse the situation.

"It ain't that serious to you 'cause it ain't your shit he slamming," Tito said as he pulled out into traffic.

For the entire ride Pop didn't say a word; he just rode in silence, caught in his own thoughts. He couldn't stand Tito, and damn sure didn't want to work with him; it took everything in his power to not to punch him in his face. He just wanted to get the job over with and go home.

"Fuck you doing? You over there crying?" Tito said just to fuck with Pop.

"Yo, just shut up and drive, damn!" Pop sucked his teeth. "You always gotta be saying something—just shut the fuck up."

Tito immediately pulled the car over to the side of the road and hopped out. "Fuck you talking to like that? Get out the car and say that shit."

"Come on let's get this shit over with," Pop said and exhaled as he slid out the passenger seat.

"Yo, y'all niggas need to chill y'all attracting mad attention, and y'all know we riding dirty," Pooh said, stepping in the middle of the two angry men. "Come on, Pop, get back in the truck and be the bigger man."

"Nah, fuck that, I'm tired of this clown-ass nigga," Pop said with his fist balled up.

Tito never took his eyes off of Pop. He wanted so badly to break his jaw, but he knew Pooh was right. "We'll handle this later," Tito said with a smirk as he slid back in the driver's seat. All three men climbed back into the Range Rover as Tito pulled back out into the street.

Twenty minutes later Tito parked across the street from the nail shop that Fresh had given him the address to.

"A'ight, look, as soon as the bitch come out we going to follow the bitch to her crib, then make her talk," Tito said, making it clear that he was in charge.

"Why don't we just catch her before she gets in her car, 'cause what if she don't go home?" Pop asked. "Then we gon' just be following her all around the town for nothing."

"Why don't you just shut the fuck up," Tito replied nastily. "We following the bitch and that's that."

"Yeah, a'ight," Pop sighed loudly. Seconds later they saw the girl they were looking for walk out of the nail shop.

"There go our girl right there," Tito said, making the engine come to life.

"Damn, she got a fat ass," Pooh said undressing the woman with his eyes.

"I still say we should just grab her now," Pop said once again.

"Shut the fuck up," Tito replied quickly as he made a U-turn and began to follow the woman. "Yeah, this nigga must be getting some money," Tito said, referring to the Lexus the woman drove.

"Yeah, we know she can't afford that shit," Pooh said from the backseat.

Twenty minutes later Tito watched the woman pull up into the driveway of a nice-looking house. "I'm about to pull up behind her; y'all go grab the bitch," Tito ordered as he zoomed the Range Rover in the driveway right behind the woman's car. Immediately, Pooh and Pop hopped out.

Tosha pulled up in her driveway and let the engine die. The only thing on her mind was a nap. She reached over and grabbed her Prada bag from off the passenger seat. Just as she was about to exit the car she saw a gray Range Rover pull up directly behind her. Tosha quickly panicked, thinking it was somebody coming to rob her. She quickly snatched the .380 that her man had given her from her purse. The first person she saw she shot.

Pow!

Pooh quickly hopped out the Range Rover and ran over to the driver's door.

"Bitch, get the fuck up out the car!" he yelled as he snatched open the door. Just as he was about to grab a handful of the woman's hair he heard the shot, saw the flash, and felt the burning. The bullet ripped through Pooh's shoulder, sending him crashing to the ground. Next in the line of fire was Pop. Tosha aimed her gun at Pop and pulled the trigger. Pop managed to duck right on time as the bullet grazed his upper back. He quickly pulled out his 9 mm and did an army roll to get out of harm's way.

Tosha hopped out of the Lexus and was about to run until she saw Tito in the driver's seat of the Range Rover smiling at her. She immediately raised her gun and emptied the clip into the windshield. Once she was out of bullets she quickly turned and tried to make a dash for her front door, but the four-inch heels she wore made it impossible to run fast.

Tito hopped out the Range Rover with his P89 already in his hand. He held it with two hands as he walked in a straight line and pulled the trigger twice. The first bullet missed, but the second one exploded in the back of Tosha's leg, stopping her dead in her tracks.

"Dumb-ass bitch," Tito huffed as he snatched the woman's Prada bag from off the ground and took out her keys. He quickly walked up to the front door and let himself in.

"I need an ambulance," Tosha cried out in pain.

Tito didn't respond; instead, he just grabbed a handful of the woman's hair and dragged her inside the house. Pop helped Pooh inside the house before he shut the door.

"Get your ass up, bitch!" Tito growled as he pulled Tosha up off the floor by her hair. The woman stood on one leg, not putting any pressure on her wounded leg. "Your man Randy, where does he keep all his shit?" Tito asked, still holding Tosha by her hair.

"What shit are you talking about?" Tosha said, still concentrating on her wounded leg.

"Now this bitch wanna be playing games," Tito mumbled as he quickly flipped Tosha on the counter by her hair. He dragged her across the whole counter. He cleaned the counter with her face, and then let her body hit the floor.

"Bitch, you must think it's a game," Tito said as he grabbed a bottle of wine from off the top of the freezer and opened it with a corkscrew.

"Get up!" Tito snarled as he pulled Tosha back up on her one leg by her hair.

"You ready to talk now?" he asked, turning the wine bottle up to his lips.

"I don't know what's going on," Tosha said in between sobs.

Tito laughed loudly before he viciously busted the wine bottle over the woman's head.

"Hey man, that's enough," Pop stepped in. "If she knew anything she would of told us by now."

"What's the matter, your stomach can't handle all this, or you don't have enough balls for this here business—which one is it?" Tito asked.

"Listen," Pop began calmly. "The bitch is already knocked out. Why don't we just sit here and wait until Randy comes home? It doesn't make sense to just keep on beating her."

"Damn, nigga, you talking like this your bitch or something." Tito smiled as he turned around and stomped Tosha in her face with his Nike boot.

Pop just shook his head, walked over to the couch, and took a seat.

"Just shut the fuck up and take notes," Tito said as he stripped the woman naked and placed her in a chair, where he began to tie her up.

"You done did all that you might as well rape her while you at it," Pop said sarcastically.

"Fuck outta here," Tito said as he spit in the woman's face. "I ain't never had to take no pussy in my life."

"Fuck all that shit," Pooh said, breathing heavily. "Y'all need to hurry up 'cause I gotta get my arm checked out."

"Suck it up, you big pussy," Tito laughed. "They don't make ganstas like they used to I see."

Tito's laughs came to a stop when Tosha began to come back around.

"Where am I and what's going on?" she mumbled, sounding drowsy.

"Today must be your lucky day, because I'm going to give you one more chance to tell me where the shit is," Tito said as he picked up a can of gasoline from over in the corner, and began pouring it on top of Tosha's head.

"No, please don't do this—I swear to God I don't know nothing about nothing," she whined as endless tears rolled down her face.

"Listen, lady, if you know anything you really need to tell us now before it's too late," Pop said, leaning in close so the woman could hear him. "Tell us something, please."

"I don't know anything about what Randy does, I swear," Tosha told him. "Please don't do this," she begged.

"I believe her," Pop said, turning to face Tito. "What sense does it make to keep torturing her if she don't know shit?"

"You know what?" Tito paused. "I think you right, let's just wait until Randy get here."

"Plus, then we might use her as bait when he gets here, you know?" Pop said as he turned around just in time to see Tito tossing a lit match on Tosha's head. The woman's body was quickly covered in flames.

Pop just looked on in amazement as he watched the woman scream as the fire burned her to death.

"What the fuck is you doing?" Pop yelled. "That shit wasn't even necessary."

"Nigga, that bitch just tried to kill you outside," Tito reminded him. "What is this bitch to you? Nothing, so shut the fuck up," he said, answering his own question.

Pop was about to reply until her heard someone come through the front door. Before he could reach for his gun, Tito had already sent a shot through Randy's leg.

"We was waiting for you," Tito said as he dragged Randy inside the house by his wrist. "Pat this mu'fucka down," Tito ordered as he walked over to the kitchen and grabbed another chair and sat it in the middle of the floor.

Pop patted the man down and removed a 9 mm from the small of the man's back.

"What the fuck y'all nigga want?" Randy asked.

"We want those bricks, cash, and whatever else you got," Tito answered simply.

"I got four bricks and about $120,000 dollars," Randy told it.

"So where it's at?" Tito asked.

"At my other crib downtown."

Tito handed Randy a piece of paper and a pen. "Write down the address and if you wasting my time it's not gonna be pretty," he said, nodding at Tosha's body that was still in flames while she was still tied up to the chair.

"Y'all didn't have to do that to her, she didn't know shit," Randy said with a murderous look in his eyes.

"Shut the fuck up!" Tito growled as he kicked Randy in his face. "Just write down the address and shut up."

Randy wrote down the address and handed the piece of paper back to Tito.

Tito took one look at the piece of paper, then turned and gave the piece of paper to Pop.

"Go check this out," Tito told him. "And don't take forever either."

"What's wrong with your legs?" Pop asked with his face screwed up. "I can watch him while you go check the address."

"Fuck outta here. I did all the work here, now it's your turn," Tito told him.

Pop snatched the paper that had the address on it from out of Tito's hand. "Where the fuck the keys at?" he asked, looking down at Randy.

"In my pocket," Randy answered.

Pop quickly took the keys and was out the door with Pooh on his heels.

About ten minutes after Pop and Pooh left Tito pulled a chair next to where Randy laid.

"I have to ask you a question," Tito began. "If you knew those blocks you put work on belonged to someone else why would you do it?"

"'cause you don't ask for blocks, you take 'em," Randy said.

"I'll give it to you, you got a lot of balls—not too much brain—but you got some balls," Tito laughed as he heard his cell phone ringing. He spoke briefly before hanging up. He slowly stood up, aimed his P89 at Randy's head, and pulled the trigger.

A week later, Pop stood on the block that Fresh had given to him not too long ago. He received stares from the local thugs; they couldn't figure out how such a young man had been given such a high promotion.

"If these fools knew better they would do better," Pop said

to himself, noticing the looks he was getting. Along with the promotion Fresh had brought him a brand-new Benz, so he could really be stunting. Pop was quickly rising in the underworld and loving every minute of the fast life. He caught on fast and became a great businessman—he paid all his workers and runners fairly unless they fucked up a pack, and he always made sure Fresh got his cut. Pop ran a smooth operation; his only problem was Tito. No matter what he did Tito always tried to outdo him. Pop wanted to shoot Tito so bad but he spared the man because he knew Fresh cared for him, but sooner or later he would have to deal with Tito, and he couldn't wait until the time came.

"Yo, I'm about to breeze, my dude, keep these niggas in line out here, B," Pop said as he gave Jason a pound. Jason was Pop's number-one lieutenant. He was in charge of collecting all the money from the workers and runners. Pop noticed the young man's hunger and decided to give him a chance of a lifetime like how Fresh had done for him. Jason was a loyal worker as well as a good friend, plus it didn't hurt that Pop trusted the young soldier.

"A'ight, I'm going to be on the block all night," Jason responded.

"Damn, you must be trying to get the hustler of the year award?" Pop joked.

"This all I got right here so you know I'm going to get this money by any means," Jason said in a matter-of-fact tone.

"I respect that you a true hustler," Pop said, answering his vibrating Nextel.

"I'm listening," he answered playfully.

"What's good, my nigga?" Instantly Pop knew it was Fresh on the other end of the phone.

"I'm chilling. I'ma 'bout to go take care of something real quick, why what's up?"

"Put that on hold until later on, I need you to come to the warehouse so I can talk to you about something," Fresh said flatly.

"A'ight I'll be there in thirty minutes," Pop replied.

"Cool," Fresh said, ending the conversation.

Pop hopped in his new Benz, leaving the whole hood staring at the sparkling rims and hearing the sound of Young Jeezy pumping through the speakers as he peeled off.

"I wonder what's so important that Fresh couldn't wait to holla at me tomorrow?" Pop asked himself as he weaved from lane to lane, doing about eighty on the highway. He parked his Benz a block away from the warehouse like he always did. Something just didn't feel right—Pop could tell by how Fresh's voice sounded on the phone.

"What's up, glad you could make it on such notice," Fresh said, giving Pop a pound.

"It's all good, so what's the big emergency?" Pop asked, taking a seat in a chair that looked very expensive.

"I got a very important job I need you to take care of for me," Fresh said, handing Pop a drink. "You the only person I trust to take care of this job." Pop could see in Fresh's eyes that he was desperate. "A'ight, what do I have to do?"

"I need you to kill Amanda for me tomorrow night," he stated plainly.

"What?" Pop asked, wondering if he had just heard correctly.

"You heard me, Pop, I said I need you to get rid of Amanda for me," Fresh stated calmly.

"Why can't you get Rusty or Tito to do it?" Pop asked, not liking the sound of the job.

"Because you are the only person I want knowing about this," Fresh said, reading Pop's facial expression. "I got everything all mapped out so you can get away clean."

"So what's the plan?" Pop asked.

"It's simple. Amanda goes to the supermarket every Sunday, so all you have to do is stake out around her building, follow her to the supermarket and clap her

"Nah, I'm going to get caught if I clap her in a supermarket parking lot—my cannon bark's too loud," Pop said, visualizing the whole shit in his head. Before Pop could say another word Fresh pulled a .380 with a silencer out of his drawer, and placed it on top of his desk. "Now what?" Fresh asked, getting impatient.

"Fuck it. It's done," Pop said, grabbing the .380 from off of the desktop.

"This is for your troubles," Fresh said, placing a brown paper bag on top of the desk.

"I got you, baby," Pop said as he took the brown paper bag and made his exit. When Pop made it back to his car he looked inside the paper bag and counted out $15,000 dollars. "All in a day's work," he said as he made the engine come alive, and fled the scene.

"Word just got back on that clown that robbed you," Rusty said, passing the blunt to Fresh.

"What's that fool's résumé?" Fresh asked, taking the blunt.

"Some stickup kid that just came home named the Truth," Rusty said, handing Fresh a picture of the stickup kid.

"You got an address for me?"

"I got it right here," Rusty answered, handing the piece of paper with the address on it to Fresh. "You want me to put Pop or Tito on the job?"

"Nah, I gotta take care of this one myself," Fresh said with a smirk on his face. "Mu'fucka thought he was just going to rob me and never hear from me again," he said, shaking his head.

"Shit can, you blame him?" Rusty asked. "People is fucked up out here right now."

"Well, he took something from the wrong mu'fucka, and now he gotta pay with his life," Fresh said, seriously.

"When you want to go handle this?" Rusty asked as he passed the blunt back to Fresh.

"The sooner the better," Fresh said, ending the conversation as he answered his ringing cell phone.

"I can't believe that nigga Fresh gave Pop his own spot to run," Tito said as he and Pooh sat in the tittie bar, getting drunk.

"Yeah, Fresh really likes that kid," Pooh slurred.

"You done put in more work than Pop, and I put in more work then both of y'all put together," Tito said with envy in his voice as he downed his drink.

"Yeah, I know but what we going to do, go head up with Fresh?" Pooh said playfully.

The only problem was Tito wasn't playing—he had big dreams that he couldn't accomplish rolling with Fresh. *Fuck it I might just have to start up my own crew*, Tito thought to himself.

"Yo, I'm going to have to catch up with you later," Pooh said, breaking up Tito's thoughts.

"A'ight, my dude, drive safe," Tito said as he gave Pooh a pound. As Pooh got up to leave, a pair of eyes followed their every move from the back of the bar.

"Ma, come here for a minute so I can scream at you for a minute," Tito said to a dark-skinned woman with a nice pair of breasts.

"If I'm coming over here I know you going to buy me a drink," Nice Titties said in a hustler's tone.

"Is this enough for your drink, tip, and number?" Tito asked, slipping the woman a hundred-dollar bill. Before the woman could answer, Tito felt somebody sit down next to him. When he turned around he was shocked to see Bamboo sitting in front of him.

"Long time no see," Bamboo said, extending his hand.

"I should pop your fuckin' head off right now, B," Tito said, looking Bamboo dead in his eyes.

"Listen, Tito, don't get ahead of yourself, I'm here to talk business with you."

Before Tito addressed Bamboo he noticed Nice Titties was still standing there. "Baby, I'm going to get up with you before I break out, a'ight," he said, dismissing the lady with nice titties.

"A'ight, just make sure you don't forget about me," she said seductively as she took her time walking off.

"Now what kind of business are you talking about?" Tito asked, sipping on his drink.

"Basically I'm about to make you a offer you can't refuse," Bamboo stated plainly.

"I'm listening, mu'fucka," Tito said, giving Bamboo his undivided attention.

"It's like this: I got mad work, but I don't got nobody to move it. I got a few small-time hustlers but I don't got that right piece to the puzzle, so I was thinking I could front you a few of them things, and we could take shit over. I could hire some workers and some muscle for you, and we just shut shit down out here. Plus, niggas won't fuck with you anyway 'cause of your street reputation. Instead of working for Fresh you could be the next Fresh," Bamboo said, really trying to sell Tito his dream.

"Your plan doesn't sound too bad," Tito said, thinking about it.

"I been planning this shit for a hot minute, there's no way this plan can go wrong—plus with me backing you up there won't be no stopping you," Bamboo said, looking over both of his shoulders as if someone was trying to eavesdrop.

"Damn, this just what the fuck I needed," Tito said to himself, wondering if the plan would work. Tito was tired of waiting for Fresh. As soon as he came home he was supposed to have his own block already waiting for him, but instead he came home only to find out that a young street punk had stolen his position.

"Oh, I forgot to tell you, if you deal with me you going to be getting the best product on the streets right now, the only thing is no funny business. If you deal with me you deal with me only. I got a hit squad on standby waiting for you if you even think about crossing me," Bamboo warned.

"Look at my face—does it look like I'm scared of your little punk-ass hit squad?" Tito asked, putting on his killer face.

"Fresh wasn't scared of my hit squad either and you see what happened to him," Bamboo said, letting out a little chuckle.

"You know what, Bamboo, I think this just might work. Give me a day or two and I'll get back to you, a'ight?"

"Take your time," Bamboo said, downing his drink. "Oh, I almost forgot to tell you. Fresh is still on my hit list, so if you got any information that will help me be able to hit him easier, I'm willing to pay for that info."

"Shit, if the price is right I'll hit him for you, that mu'fucka been shitting on me lately anyway," Tito said, meaning every word he said.

"Here's my card. Get back to me within forty-eight hours," Bamboo said as he exited the bar. Bamboo knew he could get Tito to switch to his team, because he knew how greedy and money-hungry he was. However, things would turn out even better if Tito would take care of Fresh too.

The Truth sat in his apartment playing with the new AK-47 he had just purchased, while the movie *Menace II Society* played on his TV.

"Damn, I can't wait, shoot me a nigga with this," he said, admiring his new toy. The Truth was the kind of stickup kid that took his job too serious. He loved seeing the fear on his victims' faces when he robbed them, just something about it made him feel more powerful.

"What you out here doing?" Krya asked, coming from the back room. Once she saw her man holding the AK she already knew what was up. "You know sometimes I think you love your guns more than you love me."

"So what's the problem?" the Truth joked as he blocked the pillow that Kyra threw at his head. Krya and the Truth had been together for twelve years. No matter what happen or what the Truth did Kyra always stood by her man's side.

"Let's go out and get something to eat," Kyra suggested as she sat down on the couch next to her man.

"No can do," he said, kissing Kyra on her cheek. "I gotta go out and get this money."

"You need me to drive?" Kyra asked, rubbing the back of her man's head.

"Nah, I can't have y'all out there riding with me," he replied, rubbing Kyra's stomach.

"I ain't even three months pregnant yet, I can still drive, baby."

"No, and that's final," the Truth barked. "If something happened to you I wouldn't be able to forgive myself."

"But I'm always your driver," Kyra said. "And I don't think we should switch up the program."

"Fuck the program, you ain't going and that's it," the Truth said, shutting down her plan. "And if you ask me again I'm gon' smack the shit outta you."

Kyra sucked her teeth but didn't reply. She knew that if she continued to push the issue her man would make good on his promise to smack the shit out of her. So she decided to hold her tongue.

"Come on, baby, don't act like that," he said, noticing the frown on Kyra's face. "I just can't take that kind of a chance, I love you and not only that, you carrying my son in your stomach."

"How you know it's not a girl?"

"Because it's not that's how I know," the Truth said playfully as he mushed her. "Nah, baby, but all jokes aside I want you to just chill here in the crib and relax."

"I will only on one condition," Kyra said, smiling.

"What?"

"Promise me you're going to be careful out there and make it back home to me in one piece."

"I promise I'll be extra-careful and make it back to you in one piece," he said and bent down and kissed her forehead.

"Damn, I'm hungry as fuck," Rusty said, keeping up with the traffic.

"We can eat after we take care of this clown," Fresh said, leaning back in the passenger seat with his hoodie on.

"We gon' have to be a little careful," Rusty said, keeping his eyes on the road. "My man told me this guy is a real gun fanatic."

"You know I don't give a fuck about none of that shit," Fresh said with no emotions. "He lived by the gun, now he gonna have to die by it."

Rusty pulled up a block away from the building they were headed to and let the engine die. He grabbed the Tec-9 from off the backseat. "You ready?"

"You already know," Fresh answered as he tucked his 9 mm in his waistband and slid out of the passenger seat.

Just as Fresh and Rusty was walking to the building, the Truth was walking out. He wore a skully and shades, along with a trench coat to hide his AK.

"A yo, that's him right there!" Rusty said, tapping Fresh.

The Truth turned and looked at Fresh. Immediately he knew the man from somewhere, but he couldn't figure out where. But from the look the man had in his eyes the Truth knew he was trouble. He tried to run back inside the building but it was too late.

Fresh immediately snatched his 9 mm from his waist and sent three shots in the Truth's direction. One of the shots hit him in his side, forcing him to spin around. But once he spun around his AK was already drawn.

Fresh and Rusty both quickly took cover behind a parked car as the AK lit up the streets.

The Truth dropped down to a knee and tried to apply pressure to his side to stop some of the bleeding. "Fuck," he cursed loudly from the pain that he was feeling.

"You take that side and I'ma take this side," Fresh said as he silently counted to three. Fresh ran up on the side of the car until he reached the Truth. The Truth laid on the ground holding his side with a smile on his face. "I knew you'd be back," he said, looking up at Fresh.

"I told you I would be," Fresh said as he kicked the AK-47 out of the man's reach. "The head or the chest?" he asked.

"The head," the Truth whispered, closing his eyes, preparing himself for his next life.

Fresh stood over the wounded man's body and pulled the trigger.

"Come on we gotta go," Rusty said, pulling Fresh back to the getaway car.

Upstairs Kyra sat on the couch watching *Menace II Society* when she heard three shots go off followed by several more. Immediately her heart sank. All she could think about was her man. "Please don't let nothing happen to my man," she prayed as she quickly threw on some clothes and flew out of the house. Once Kyra made it downstairs she dropped to her knees when she saw her man laid out in a pool of his own blood. "No baby, why didn't you just let me come with you?" she cried, mad at herself for letting him change her mind. When the ambulance arrived and she watched them cover her man's body with the white sheet, she immediately passed out.

Chapter Thirteen

"I can't believe this mu'fucka," Amanda huffed as she ironed her shirt. "He got some damn nerve to be acting like this toward me, when he the one that's cheating. If anybody should be mad it's me."

"Yeah, but you know how guys act, they all think they can have they cake and eat it too," Melissa told her sister. "But if I felt or thought Pop was cheating on me I would be hurt, but I would leave him."

"I been wanting to leave Fresh," Amanda said as a tear escaped her eye. "But I can't 'cause I just love him so much," she said as she broke down in tears.

"I understand," Melissa said as she hugged her sister tightly and rubbed her back while she let it all out.

"Everything Fresh has ever asked me to do I've done it without him ever having to ask me twice," Amanda said, not understanding why he was treating her the way he was. "He could of at least came and bailed me out of jail himself."

"Well, you never know he might have been busy," Melissa said, trying to make up an excuse for him.

"That mu'fucka wasn't busy," Amanda said, waving her hand and making a gesture. "At least come pick me up and let me know everything is going to be all right or something."

"Yeah, I feel you," Melissa told her as she just continued to listen to her sister vent.

"As a matter of fact as soon as we get back from the supermarket I'm going over to the warehouse to talk to Fresh, and tell him how much I really love him and let him know that I want to work it out. Fuck that, I ain't letting my man go that easy so some other bitch can have him. Fuck that," Amanda said as the two women high-fived-each other.

"Meet me downstairs, I'm going to get the car," Melissa said, making her exit.

Pop sat staked out in front of Amanda's building for half the day before she finally stepped out the building. He watched closely as a Honda pulled up to the curb forty-five minutes later, and Amanda hopped in the passenger seat.

"This wasn't part of the plan," Pop said to himself as he turned on his car and began to follow the Honda. Pop made sure he stayed at least three cars behind the Honda. Ten minutes later he followed the Honda into a supermarket's parking lot.

"I'll just wait until Amanda comes out the supermarket and pop her and her friend," Pop said to himself as he screwed the silencer on the .380. Pop's heart instantly leaped up into his throat when he saw Melissa slide out of the driver's side of the Honda.

"Fuck," Pop yelled, banging the steering wheel. He didn't have a backup plan so it wasn't much he could do.

"What the fuck are you doing here, baby?" Pop asked himself as he watched Melissa and Amanda disappear inside the supermarket. Pop couldn't believe what he was seeing. Now that Melissa was there the game had changed, and so did the rules. Melissa would now have to go along with her sister.

***

"I feel much better, I think I just needed to get out of the house for a second and get some fresh air," Amanda said as she and Melissa stood in the checkout line.

"Y'all going to be fine," Melissa said, placing their items on the register's counter.

"I just need to talk to Fresh, I will feel much better once I just talk to him," Amanda said to herself as she watched the cashier ring up their groceries.

Twenty-five minutes later Pop saw Melissa and Amanda strolling out of the supermarket pushing a shopping cart. Pop quickly threw on his hockey mask and drew the strings on his hoodie as he exited the vehicle. As he got closer to the two women he made sure he walked with his head down so his mask wasn't visible.

Melissa and Amanda put their groceries in the trunk, never noticing the masked man creeping up behind them. Once Pop got in shooting range, he quickly aimed his .380 at Amanda's head and pulled the trigger. The first shot hit Amanda in the back of her head, causing her to slump halfway inside the trunk. The next two shots sunk into the lifeless woman's body. Before Melissa got her lungs ready to scream, Pop put the hot silencer to her head.

"Go ahead and scream. I dare you!" Pop growled, looking at Melissa's pretty face coated in specks of blood. "Don't fuckin' move, bitch!" Pop said, keeping the .380 trained on Melissa's chest. With his free hand Pop tossed the rest of Amanda's body in the trunk.

"Two choices: Get in the trunk or I put you in!" Pop stated nonchalantly. Without thinking twice Melissa climbed in the trunk on top of her sister's dead body. Pop quickly slammed the trunk closed and power-walked back to his getaway car. Once inside the car he stormed out of the parking lot like it wasn't no tomorrow. "Fuck, I wonder if she recognized my voice?" Pop thought out loud as he snatched off his mask, weaving from lane to lane. Pop felt bad about the whole situation; he loved Melissa and didn't want to hurt her, but he had to do what he had to do. Deep down inside he knew he should have shot Melissa also, but he just couldn't do it. Pop double-parked the getaway car on a quiet block and walked to the next avenue so he could flag down a cab. He sat in the cab, replaying the whole situation in his head. His thoughts were rudely interrupted when he felt his Nextel vibrating.

"Yo," Pop answered.

"How's it looking?" Fresh asked.

"Everything went according to plan," Pop replied.

"A'ight, hit me back later," Fresh said, ending the call, not wanting to talk that kind of business over the phone. When Pop got out of the cab, he went straight to the bootleg liquor spot, and got himself something to sip on.

As he headed back to the projects Pop felt his Nextel vibrating once again. He looked at the caller ID and saw that it was Nika.

"Hey, baby, what's up?"

"Nothing, I just finished cooking dinner, and I was just wondering if you would be able to join me tonight?" she asked.

"Yeah, I'm walking in the building right now, I'll be upstairs in like two minutes," Pop said as he lost his signal as he stepped on the pissy elevator. Immediately when Nika laid her eyes on Pop she could tell that something was wrong. "Baby, what's wrong?" she asked.

"Nothing, baby, I'm just a little tired that's all," he lied.

"Okay, I'm going to make our plates, go wash your hands," Nika said over her shoulder as she disappeared into the kitchen.

"Yo, this steak is the bomb," Pop stated, washing his steak down with some gin and juice.

"Mu'fuckas are going crazy out here. You heard some bitch got killed at the supermarket tonight?" Nika asked.

"Get the fuck out of here," Pop said, acting unaware of the situation.

"Yeah, somebody shot some Dominican bitch and then tossed her in the trunk along with her sister. It's all over the news," Nika said, shaking her head. "That's fucked up—people can't even go grocery shopping without getting killed."

"So the guy killed two Dominican girls?" Pop asked, playing it off.

"Nah, he only killed one, so I don't know what that's all about, all I know is mu'fucka is crazy," Nika said, filling her glass with an equal amount of gin and juice.

"What is this world coming to," Pop added as he felt his Nextel vibrating.

"Yo," he answered.

"Why the fuck you didn't tell me Melissa was at the scene tonight?" Fresh barked into the receiver.

"I didn't think it mattered," Pop answered.

"Nigga, are you stupid? She's a fuckin' witness, not to mention she saw what happened at the club. I'm the only mu'fucka the fingers are going to get pointed at. Especially since you killed one and not the other. Why the fuck didn't you just kill that bitch?" Fresh asked venomously.

Pop got up and went in the bedroom before he answered. "I don't know why I didn't think this shit was going to fall back on you. My job was to do Amanda, and that's what I did. I didn't even know Melissa was going to be there."

"I'm going to try to talk to her but if it looks fishy then she's going to have to go simple as that," Fresh said.

"Not a problem," Pop said, sounding a little shaky.

"A'ight, I'm going to scream at you later, I'm about to head to the hospital so shit don't look out of place smell me?"

"I can dig it, keep me posted," Pop said, pressing no on his cell phone. Pop knew he had fucked up, but he didn't want to kill Melissa unless he had to, but from how Fresh was talking he knew Melissa would have to go soon.

"Is everything all right?" Nika asked, stepping into the bedroom.

"Yeah, I'm cool, just a little tired. I think I'm going to lay down for a little while," Pop answered.

"I know just what you need," Nika said, removing her robe and closing the door behind her. Pop watched as Nika slowly made her way over to him. He was about to say something, but Nika quickly hushed him.

"Shh," she whispered as she placed one finger on his lips, then began removing Pop's pants. He had built-up stress in him for the past few days and Nika knew just how to get it out of him. First, she planted soft, wet kisses all over his dick as she felt his manhood rise in her hand.

"Stand up," Nika ordered as she dropped down to her knees.

"Why, baby?" Pop asked, liking the position he was already in.

"Because I want you to fuck my mouth, daddy," Nika whined as she continued to jerk his dick in her hand. Pop quickly obeyed his woman's command as he quickly stood up and began to stroke Nika's mouth at a steady pace. Pop enjoyed watching himself slide in and out of Nika's warm, wet mouth.

As soon as he felt himself getting ready to cum he quickly began to speed up his strokes until he exploded in Nika's mouth. Once that was all said and done the two fell asleep in each other's arms.

Chapter Fourteen

"I'm glad to see you made the right choice," Bamboo said, giving Tito a pound.

"Yeah, it's simple mathematics, you dig? One plus one equals two, I can make more money with you so that's what it is," Tito responded as he took a seat on the couch.

"We about to do it real big, I hope you ready," Bamboo said, rubbing his hands together.

"I was born ready, my dude," Tito said, looking at the two bricks sitting on the counter.

"I'm going to give you two bricks to start you out with a'ight? Move them shits then I'll really break you off with the real shit a'ight?"

"I can dig it," Tito said, placing the two bricks in a bag.

"Yo, this my man, Rocky, right here," Bamboo said, pointing to the three-hundred-pound beast standing next to him. "His assignment is to go everywhere with you just in case something pops off or whatever."

"I don't do bodyguards," Tito said flatly.

"You sure? You never know—he might just come in handy, you need somebody shot or something. Now you don't have to get your hands dirty," Bamboo replied.

"The only bodyguard I need is right here," Tito said, flashing the handle of his P89.

"You really need to lose that goon mentality, you about to

be making a lot of money, more money, more problems, more enemies," Bamboo said, trying to school the youngin' on a few things.

"Call it what you want but I roll solo," Tito said, tossing the duffel bag over his shoulder

"If you need anything, Tito, you know where to find me."

"A'ight, baby, good looking," Tito answered as he broke out.

"Knucklehead is going to have to learn the hard way," Bamboo said, shaking his head.

"It's hotter than a mu'fucka out here today. Cops been riding by left and right," Jason said, giving Pop a quick rundown on what had been going on.

"A'ight, just try to get the customers in and out so shit don't look too suspect," Pop stated smoothly.

"Oh, yeah, you heard about your man?" Jason asked

"Who that?" Pop asked curiously.

"Tito."

"What about that cocksucker?" Pop asked carelessly.

"My cousin out in Brooklyn said that Tito out there pumping his own shit," Jason informed.

"Get the fuck out of here!" Pop said, not believing his right-hand man.

"Nah, I'm dead-ass, my cousin said Tito been taking over niggas spots all over in B.K."

"I don't believe that, Brooklyn niggas don't fold that easy," Pop said, not believing the gossip.

"I don't know how he's doing it but it's getting done," Jason said, lighting up a Newport.

"I wonder if Fresh knows about this," Pop thought out loud.

"Probably not, you know Tito is a sneaky mu'fucka," Jason reminded him.

"That clown better keep that bullshit out in Brooklyn 'cause if he come up here with that bullshit it ain't no talking, I'm straight popping off," Pop stated plainly.

"I can dig it," Jason said, giving Pop a pound.

Before Pop could say another word he felt his Nextel vibrating. He looked at his phone and saw Melissa's name flashing across the screen.

"Yooo," he answered.

"Pop, it's me, Melissa," she said, crying into the receiver.

"What's wrong, baby? I came to your house the other day but you weren't home," Pop lied.

"Somebody murdered Amanda the other night that's why I haven't been home, I know you heard about it," she sobbed.

"Please tell me you lying about Amanda?" Pop said, playing it off.

"No Pop, I'm dead serious," Melissa cried.

"So where are you now?" he asked.

"I'm at my cousin's house, but I'm about to go out of town for a minute so I can be with my family for a while, but I can't leave until I see you first," Melissa said through a sniffle.

"A'ight, so where do you want to meet me at?" he asked.

"Umm, I'll meet you at ten o'clock at that hotel you took me to last week in the Bronx," Melissa answered.

"A'ight I'll be there," Pop told her.

"Okay, I'll see you later," Melissa replied.

"A'ight," Pop said, ending the conversation. Pop looked at his watch and saw that it was 9:25. "Yo, I'm about to get up out of here," Pop said as he gave Jason a pound.

"A'ight, Pop. Holla at me tomorrow."

Pop hung up the phone but before he could reach his Benz he got stopped by two little kids.

"Pop, can you buy us a soda?" one of the kids asked.

"Y'all brothers ate anything tonight?" Pop asked, digging in his pocket.

"Yeah, we had some cookies earlier," one of the kids answered

"Some cookies," Pop said, quoting the young kid. "Here, B. Y'all go get some chicken from the chicken spot down the street," he said, handing both kids a twenty-dollar bill. "And go straight home when y'all finish 'cause it's getting late!" he yelled over his shoulder as he hopped in his Benz.

"Fuckin' no-good parents," Pop mumbled out loud as he started up the Benz and peeled off. He had no idea what he was going to say when he saw Melissa face-to-face, or how she would be acting, but he had to see her in person just so shit didn't look suspect. When Pop got close to the hotel, he pulled out his Nextel and called her.

"Yo, I'm a block away from the hotel, where you at?" he asked.

"I'm right here in the front waiting for you," Melissa answered.

"Okay, I'll be there in one minute," he said and then hung up.

When Melissa saw the Benz stop right in front of her, she quickly slid in the passenger seat.

"Hey, baby," she said as she kissed Pop on his cheek.

The ride around the corner to the hotel was a quiet one. Pop didn't know what to say so he just said nothing.

"Yo, let me get a room for two days," Pop said, pulling out a big wad of cash and paying the desk clerk.

As soon as Pop and Melissa stepped inside the hotel room, she started spilling her guts. "I don't know who could have done this shit," she said, breaking down in tears.

***

"Slow down for a minute, and start from the beginning," Pop said, trying to calm Melissa down.

"Me and Amanda was coming out of the supermarket minding our business," she said, sobbing. "When out of nowhere some guy wearing a hockey mask came and shot Amanda four times like it was nothing," Melissa said, her crying only getting worse.

"Then what happen?" Pop asked innocently.

"Then he threw her body in the trunk and put the gun to my head, and told me to get in the trunk with my sister's dead body," Melissa said in tears.

"So what did you do?" Pop asked.

"What you think I did? I got in the mu'fuckin' trunk!" she said excitedly.

"That's crazy—if I find out who did this shit I'm definitely going to catch a case," Pop said, talking with his hands. "That's some foul shit."

"No baby, I don't want you getting in no trouble," Melissa said, wiping her tears away with the back of her hand.

"Who the fuck would do some shit like that?" Pop asked, stroking the back of Melissa's head. "Well, you're safe now, you know I'm not going to let nothing happen to you," he said, holding her in his arms.

"I love you, Pop. You're the only man I will ever love. Nobody could ever take your place," Melissa whispered as she unbuckled Pop's belt. He wanted to tell Melissa what really happened but he knew he couldn't. The only thing the truth would do would leave Melissa with a broken heart.

Pop's thoughts were quickly interrupted when he felt Melissa's hand creep to his jeans and pull out his thickness. Her soft, wet lips made contact with his penis and made his toes curl instantly. He grabbed a handful of Melissa's hair as he began to stroke her mouth. After ten minutes of sucking, Melissa was ready for the dick. She quickly snatched her clothes off like a wild, caged animal.

Once Melissa got her pants off she violently pushed Pop on the bed and hopped on top of him.

"Tell me how bad you want this pussy," she said, letting her titties hang directly in front of Pop's face.

"I'm about to tear you up," he growled as he grabbed one of Melissa's pretty titties and placed it in his mouth like it was a pacifier. He then smoothly slid Melissa's thong over to the side and entered her sopping wet pussy. He made sure he cupped both of her ass cheeks so that they were spread apart as he help guide Melissa's nice-sized ass up and down his pole, nice and slow.

"Oh, *papi*," Melissa moaned, loving every stroke. She opened her legs as far as they could so that she could feel every inch of Pop's dick. Her legs were so far spread that it looked like she was doing the split while still riding him.

"Oh, shit, I'm about to cum," Pop moaned as he tried to hold back as long as he could. Melissa quickly hopped up and began sucking the shit out of Pop's dick until he filled her mouth with his fluids.

"Oh," Pop moaned and groaned as Melissa continued to peck away at his dick.

"Who's that bitch?" Melissa said, smiling as she wiped her mouth with the back of her hand.

"You that bitch, baby," Pop said, out of breath, as he laid sprawled across the bed.

Chapter Fifteen

"Is that him right there?" Tito asked one of his flunkies as he pointed to a man standing on the corner.

"Yeah, that's him," the flunky answered surely.

Tito slowly slid out of the driver's seat of his Lexus, making his way over to the corner followed by his flunky.

"Yo, my man, ya name Carl?" Tito asked, approaching the man standing on the corner.

"Yeah, why, who wants to know?" Carl responded, looking Tito up and down.

"Yo, my man! Is this your block? I need to speak to the mu'fucka who's running this shit," Tito stated harshly.

"You talking to him now," Carl replied, not afraid to get ignorant if he had to.

"Listen, I hear your block is going some good numbers," Tito said as he took a short pause before he continued. "Long story short, I need in."

"Nigga, you must be crazy! This my shit!" Carl said, raising his voice.

"Listen, either you take my package or you can step the fuck off. Simple as that," Tito said, sounding smooth.

"This is my block and I ain't about to start sharing it with nobody!" Carl said, standing his ground.

"Brother, either you take my package or I send my shooters up here every day and make this shit hot. Then you won't be getting no money. With me, at least you'll be getting forty percent and giving up sixty, so let me know how you wanna play it," Tito said, slipping a blunt between his lips. Carl didn't respond as he weighed the options in his head. Tito took Carl's silence as acceptance. "That's what I thought. Carl, my man will be up here tomorrow with that package. Sixty-forty split." Tito chuckled as he walked back to his Lexus.

Tito knew if he threatened Carl to make his block hot he would fold like a paper bag, plus Carl knew Tito wasn't bluffing. "This shit is too fuckin' easy," Tito said to himself as he headed to the Bronx to go pick up one of his girlfriends. Tito wasn't playing no games, if you were making money he was definitely coming to see you. His name really started buzzing after he shot this big-time drug dealer that wasn't willing to share his real estate. He was making more money than he ever imagined. Life couldn't get any better than it already was. Tito even went out and bought himself a big chain that had *Tito* spelled on it in diamonds, along with a diamond flooded bracelet with the pinky ring to match. He also went out and bought himself a brand-new cherry-red convertible Porsche. Every other day Tito found himself getting pulled over by the cops due to him being so flashy, but he didn't care. That's just how Tito was; you could love it or hate it. Tito zoomed in and out of the highway lanes doing ninety in a fifty-five speed zone, when he heard his cell phone ringing.

"Yo, who this?" he asked.

"It's me, Fresh."

"Oh, what's good, my nigga?" Tito asked, keeping his eyes on the road.

"Come to the warehouse, I need to talk to you," Fresh stated, holding his cards to his chest and revealing nothing in his tone.

"A'ight I'll be there tomorrow," Tito said nonchalantly.

"Nah, I need to see you right now, B," Fresh said, slamming the phone down in Tito's ear.

"Bitch-ass nigga," Tito mumbled as he closed his phone.

Tito parked his new Porsche in front of the warehouse. "What's good, you wanted to see me?" Tito asked, helping himself to a seat.

"What's really good with you, B?" Fresh asked in a firm tone.

"What you talking about?" Tito asked, cleaning his nails.

"I hear you in business for yourself now." Fresh looked at Tito for a comment.

"Yeah, you know I had to step out, and spread my wings. We born to fly, you know?" Tito said in his best pimp voice.

"So who's promoting you?"

"Excuse me?"

"Who's supplying you?" Fresh growled, getting upset.

"Names aren't important," Tito said nonchalantly.

"It's like that now, Tito?" Fresh asked with ice in his voice.

"It's just like that, B, I'm supposed to just starve waiting for you? I don't think so, you feeding that nigga Pop more than you feeding me what kind of shit is that? That's some sucker shit, I'm the one who been holding you down for years not him."

"Listen Tito it doesn't—" Fresh said.

"No, nigga, you listen," Tito barked, cutting Fresh off. "I put in way more work than anybody on this team, and all you did was shit on me, who the fuck is Pop? Nobody!" Tito said, answering his own question. "Next time I see that nigga that's my word, I'ma pop that nigga."

"Listen to me carefully, Tito. You are no longer welcome in

this family. You ain't shit but a disloyal flunky," Fresh said, staring Tito dead in his eyes. "I'm only going to tell you this one time: get your peoples off my corners or it's going to be a problem. What, you thought you was just gonna muscle your way on everybody's corners without me finding out? Those last three block you took over in the Bronx belong to me, and I'd appreciate it if you got your peoples off those three blocks before I do," Fresh warned.

"No problem," Tito responded drily. "Can I go now?"

"Get the fuck out of here, next time you don't get no pass. Rusty, show this mu'fucka to the door," Fresh ordered.

"Not a problem," Rusty stated as he escorted Tito to the exit.

"Don't touch me, mu'fucka, I know how to walk," Tito jerked his arm from Rusty's grip. "Get the fuck off me."

Once Tito made his exit Fresh started up again. "This mu'fucka got a lot of nerves," he said out loud.

"If you want me to clip that nigga just say the word," Rusty stated plainly.

"Nah, I got something even better for that clown," Fresh stated flatly, leaning back in his chair.

"Yo, this nigga Fresh tried to get fly with me earlier," Tito said heatedly, not liking how Fresh came at him.

"Word? What happened?" Bamboo asked.

"Nothing, he just mad 'cause I'm out here getting paper like it's the eighties all over again, you dig," Tito said, pouring himself a drink.

"So you gonna take care of him or do I need to send out my hit squad again?" Bamboo asked, knowing firsthand that Fresh was going to be hard to kill.

"Nah, I'll take care of him myself," Tito responded quickly. "He ain't as strong as he used to be."

"A'ight, once it's done I'll have twenty thousand waiting for you," Bamboo told him.

"Now you speaking my language," Tito said, finishing up his drink.

"I'll see you next week, my dude," Tito said as he disappeared out the front door.

Chapter Sixteen

"What's wrong, Pop, you haven't even touched your breakfast?" Nika asked.

"Nah, I was just thinking I want to set something up for the kids," Pop said distantly as if he were deep in thought.

"What kids?" Nika asked curiously.

"Kids, period. I want to open up something that would keep kids out of the streets, like a gym or playground or something, you dig? Kids shouldn't have to grow up like I did," he said taking a sip from his orange juice.

"Well, whatever you want to do just let me know and I'll do my best to help," she told him.

"A'ight, I'm going to think of something 'cause too many black kids are turning to the streets and ending up in jail," Pop said in deep thought.

"Well, it's better to lead by example, you can't tell kids not to live the street life and you out living it," Nika stated plainly . . . honestly.

"Yeah, I know I was going to try to surprise you, but fuck it—at the end of the month I'm moving to Miami to start my life over from scratch, and I was hoping you would join me," Pop said seriously. "I been thinking about this shit for a long time now."

"Get the fuck outta here," Nika said, not believing a word Pop spoke.

"Nah, I'm dead-ass . . . word to everything I love," he said seriously.

"Oh, of course I will," she said, jumping into his arms.

"Yeah, baby, I got enough money to open up a few businesses, so we can live comfortably, plus the money I make this month I'll use that to open up something for the kids," he told her.

"That plan sounds great, Pop, I never been to Miami before," Nika said with excitement.

"Me either," Pop replied quickly.

"It's time to leave New York 'cause it's too much shit going on out here, plus I'm in too deep in this drug game. I'm either going to end up dead or in jail, and I'm too young for all that, you know what I'm saying?" Pop stated plainly.

"You right, you need to move to a spot where don't nobody know who you are," Nika agreed.

"You just make sure you keep your mouth shut, and don't tell nobody," he joked.

"What about my mother?" Nika asked.

"You can tell her a day before we leave, a'ight?"

"Okay, baby, sounds cool to me. I'm about to go jump in the shower real quick," Nika said, removing her clothes right in front of Pop.

"A'ight, baby," he responded as he answered his vibrating Nextel.

"Fresh, what's good, my dude?"

"I'm chilling, I need to holla at you so when you get a chance swing by the warehouse for a second," Fresh said in a mellow tone.

"A'ight, my nigga, I'll be there in like an hour."

"A'ight I'll see you then," Fresh said, ending the conversation.

"I hope Fresh got a job for me, because I could use the extra money," Pop said to himself as he hopped in his Benz and headed to the warehouse. He didn't know what he was going to do for the kids yet, but whatever it was he knew it was going to cost.

As Pop drove to the warehouse he looked out the window and noticed all the little kids playing outside. "Damn, I have to hurry up and come up with a good idea for these kids," Pop said as he pulled up a block away from the warehouse. "What's goodie?" Pop asked, giving Rusty a pound.

"You know, regular shit," Rusty responded as he closed the door behind Pop.

"Pop, have a seat, I got a job but I knew nobody would want this job more than you," Fresh said, pouring Pop a drink.

"So what do I have to do?" Pop asked.

"This cocksucker Tito has got to go, and I know how much you hate him so I thought you might want this job, I saved it just for you," Fresh said nonchalantly.

"Yeah, I'll take care of it," Pop answered flatly. Pop didn't really want to hurt people any more. The reason he started hurting people in the first place was so he could get paid. Now that he was paid he didn't have the hunger inside of him to really hurt people any more, but he took the job 'cause he needed the extra money, and he couldn't stand Tito. After what Pop did to Amanda he no longer had that fire inside of him, like back when he was broke and hungry. Now that he had money the more he hurt people the less it made sense.

"It's about fuckin' time you let me get at this clown," he said, feeling a little saucy already. Pop didn't like doing jobs anymore, but since Tito was the victim, he didn't have a problem with this one.

***

Tito sat in the passenger seat of the Honda staring out the window, patiently waiting to see the person he was looking for. In the driver's seat sat one of his flunkies.

"Yo, you sure this nigga gonna show up?" the flunky asked, looking over at Tito.

"Yeah, this where he always be at," Tito replied as he took a long drag from his piff. He was waiting for a local hustler who went by the name Trees. About a week before Tito approached Trees with his proposition and he turned it down, so now he had to pay.

Trees stepped out of his building with a frown on his face. He had just got finished beating up his baby mother 'cause he was looking through her phone and found a few male numbers in there.

"Bitches get on my last nerve," Trees mumbled as he looked down at his cell phone.

"Yo, there go your boy right there," the flunky, said pointing.

"Pull up on that nigga slow," Tito said, cocking back his P89 and sitting it on his lap.

Trees sat with his phone in his hand texting. He never noticed the Honda rolling up on him.

The flunky pulled the Honda up directly in front of the victim.

"A yo, my man," Tito called out. His arm hung out the window, revealing the P89.

When Trees saw Tito he almost shitted on himself. "Yo, yo chill," he pleaded as he began to backpedal.

Tito quickly raised his arm and let off five shots. Each shot found a home somewhere in Tree's body.

Once Tito stuck his arm back inside the window, his flunky gunned the engine, fleeing the crime scene.

Jason stood on the block, watching the fiends come and

go. "That's right get that money," Jason said to himself as he watched his workers trade the fiends crack for money.

"There go my nigga right there," Jason mumbled when he saw the Benz pull up to the curb.

"How it's looking out here, B?" Pop asked as he stepped out of his Benz and gave Jason a pound.

"Yo, the block jumping like the playoffs right now," Jason boasted.

"That's what I like to hear, B," Pop said as he stepped in the bodega to grab him something to drink. "Yo, J., come take a ride with me real quick," Pop said, reappearing out of the store.

"What's on ya mind, Pop?"

"Nothing I just want to let you know that you been doing a real good job out here on these streets," Pop said, pulling out into traffic.

"Come on, Pop, you know I'm going to do what I have to do to get this paper by any means necessary, baby," Jason boasted proudly.

"Yeah, I know, that's what I need to talk to you about, B," Pop said with one hand on the steering wheel, "I might be leaving soon."

"Where you going?" Jason asked, turning his neck so fast he saw Pop flinch.

"I don't know, I might be leaving town for a while real soon," Pop revealed.

"You don't even have to tell me, I know you going to have to shut the block down, right?" Jason asked.

"Nah, actually I was going to pass the shit over to you," he said as he watched a Kool-Aid smile appear on Jason's face.

"Get the fuck out of here, you serious?" Jason asked in disbelief.

"Yeah, you been doing such a good job I decided to keep the money in the family," Pop told him.

"That's what's up, so when you plan on leaving?"

"Probably at the end of the month, but the only thing is for this last month I'm not going to be able to pay you 'cause I need this money to move, but once I'm gone you going to be getting all the money, you dig?" Pop stated.

"Yeah, I'm with that, whatever I can do to help I'm going to do it," Jason said seriously.

"Yeah, baby, four more weeks, and I'm out of here," Pop said out loud as he and Jason cruised around Harlem.

Chapter Seventeen

Week One

The day seemed to drag along as Pop sat in a black Honda one block away from where Tito stood with a few of his soldiers. Pop was trying to see if Tito had a regular routine so it would be easier to erase the man, instead of getting into a reckless shoot-out with Tito in the middle of the street.

"Yo, I'm going to get up with y'all fools later," Tito said as he hopped in his Porsche and pulled out into traffic. For the whole ride he noticed the Honda tailing him. Pop made sure he stayed at least three cars behind the Porsche, so Tito wouldn't spot him.

"This mu'fucka must think I'm stupid," Tito said, looking through his rearview mirror at the black Honda. "This what the fuck I'm talking about, let's get it poppin'," he said, keeping his eyes on the road as he cocked back his P89 and placed it on his lap. Pop stopped two blocks away as he saw the Porsche stop in front of an apartment building. Seconds later Pop noticed a nice-looking woman come strolling out of the building. He watched as she slid in the passenger seat of the Porsche.

"Hey, baby," Nice Titties said as she kissed Tito on the cheek.

"What's good? I see you looking sexy as usual," Tito said,

taking a second to look at the woman's body before he continued. "What's good, you want to go grab something to eat?"

"Sure, why not?" Nice Titties answered shrugging her shoulders. She didn't care what they did. She was just happy to be
around the up-and-coming street hustler. As soon as Tito
pulled off, Nice Titties' head quickly disappeared down into
Tito's lap.

Tito almost lost control of the vehicle when he felt the
young lady's lips wrapped around his love stick. He watched
her head bob up and down in a slow but steady pace. Twenty
minutes later Tito parallel-parked across the street from a
fancy restaurant. Before he stepped out the Porsche he made
sure he placed his P89 in his waistband so he could reach
it quicker when necessary. When Pop saw Tito and his lady
friend step out of the vehicle, he made his move. He quickly
threw on his hockey mask followed by his hoodie as he cocked
back his .45 and hopped out the Honda. He walked softly but
at a fast pace, trying not to be detected.

"You know you my favorite girl, right?" Tito lied, putting
his arm around Nice Titties.

As Tito continued lying to his female friend, he slowly
slid his P89 from his waistband and clutched it tight in his
hand. When Pop got close enough to his target his heart
began to pound in anticipation of what was about to pop off.
He quickly aimed his .45 at Tito's back and pulled the trigger.

As Tito walked something told him to turn around now.
When Tito turned around he saw a man in a hockey mask
holding a gun. Instantly, his survival skills kicked in full-blast.
Tito quickly pulled Nice Titties in front of him. Her body jerked
back from the impact of the multiple shots that exploded in
her chest.

Tito tried to continue to use Nice Titties' body as a human

shield but her lifeless body was too heavy for him to continue to hold up. Without thinking twice he quickly tossed the woman's lifeless body to the ground like a rag doll as he dashed into the restaurant, throwing three reckless shots over his shoulder in the process.

Pop dodged the three shots as he followed his target inside the restaurant. When all the rich white people saw the Dominican man run in the restaurant with a gun in his hand, they immediately started to panic.

"Oh my God, he's got a gun!" a white woman screamed out, immediately causing a mini-stampede to form.

When Pop entered the restaurant, he saw Tito trying to blend in with the white crowd. Without hesitation Pop aimed his .45 at the crowd, sending three shots in their direction.

As Tito tried to find a way out of the restaurant, he noticed a white woman next to him drop to the floor from a bullet from the gunman.

Tito found himself running into a dead end. He quickly turned toward the window and sent two shots from his Ruger into the thick glass. The two bullets went straight through the glass causing it to shatter but not break. When Tito saw the gunman getting closer, he ran full speed toward the window. Once close enough, he jumped through the shattered glass, landing onto the street.

"Fuck!" Pop yelled, knowing he couldn't continue the chase because the police would be there in no time.

When Pop made it outside he quickly ran around the corner and removed his hockey mask and hoodie as he ran to the next avenue to catch a cab. As Pop sat in the cab he saw several police cars storming past him, headed in the opposite direction. "That was a close one," he said to himself as he closed his eyes for the rest of the ride. All he could think about was how close he had come blowing it all by getting locked up.

Seven hours later, Tito showed back up to the crime scene. "It's on and poppin' now," he said to himself as he hopped back in his Porsche and peeled off.

Tito didn't know who had tried to kill him but he knew Fresh had something to do with it. He drove down the street like a madman who just lost his best friend; the only thing on his mind was getting even with Fresh. Tito had a street reputation to uphold, and he planned on doing his best to do that.

"These mu'fucka must be crazy," Tito laughed loudly before he continued. "Sending a fuckin' rookie to try to smoke me, it probably was that young street punk Pop," he said out loud, replaying the scene over again in his head as he pulled up in front of his house. No matter what Tito did he just couldn't stop thinking about the situation. "Fuck that," he said as he walked to his closet and pulled out a black hoodie. "These fools done fucked with the wrong one," he growled as he reloaded his P89 and headed right back out the door. Instead of hopping in his Porsche, this time Tito hopped in his all-black Acura.

He took seven minutes to roll up a blunt before he finally pulled out of his driveway. When Tito finally made it to his destination, he slowly rolled down his window and grabbed his P89.

"Now mu'fucka wanna be hiding and shit," Tito said out loud as he noticed all the lights in Fresh's warehouse were off.

Once Tito was directly in front of the warehouse, he stuck his arm out the window and let a whole clip full of fireballs spit from his cannon. The bullets shattered every window in the warehouse, and left big dents in the places that couldn't be shattered.

"Fuck boys," Tito snarled as he left the smell of burned rubber in the air. He knew that there was nobody in the warehouse, but his plan was to send a message, and that message was, let the war begin!

Chapter Eighteen

Week Two

As Pop stepped out his Benz he immediately didn't like the looks of the dark streets. "Yo, hurry up," Pop told Nika as he checked the pistol in his waist, making sure the gun didn't protrude.

Ever since the hit on Tito hadn't gone through as planned, Pop had been very paranoid, especially when he was with Nika, because he knew if anything happened to her because of him, he wouldn't be able to live with himself.

"Is everything all right, baby?" Nika asked, noticing that the look on Pop's face was a look of worry.

"Yeah, everything is cool," Pop answered quickly, looking in the opposite direction. Nika knew something was wrong, but she left the issue alone because she knew Pop had a lot on his mind, and the last thing she wanted was Pop to not have a clear mind, so close to them leaving the city that never sleeps.

"Yo, let me get a table for two," Pop said as the nice waitress escorted him and Nika to their table.

"Here you go," the waitress said, handing the couple two menus as they took their seats.

"I'll be back to take your order in a second," the waitress said, giving Pop a sexy look before she disappeared in the kitchen.

"You know that bitch or something?" Nika asked snaking her neck.

"Come on, don't start that bullshit tonight, we came to have a good time, so let's just enjoy ourselves," Pop said, not wanting Nika to mess up the night.

"Well that bitch better act like she got some mu'fuckin' sense when she come back this way," Nika said, sucking her teeth.

"Calm down, baby, let's just talk about what we going to do for these kids, and have a good time," Pop said, trying to change the subject. "I was thinking about opening up an after-school center or something like that. What you think about that, baby?"

"That sounds cool but if you do that then you probably going to have to do that in Miami instead of New York," Nika suggested.

"Yeah, you right," he agreed.

"Baby, your idea sounds great," Nika said, placing her hand on top of Pop's hand. Before she could say another word the waitress reappeared at the table.

"Y'all ready to order yet? she huffed.

"Yeah, let me get a steak, some French fries, and a bottle of champagne," Pop said, handing the waitress back the menu.

"And will you be having anything?" the waitress asked, rolling her eyes at Nika.

"Yeah, I'll have a chicken breast, some yellow rice, and a salad, thank you," Nika said, looking the waitress up and down as she handed her back the menu. The waitress gave Nika one last dirty look before she disappeared back into the kitchen. "If this bitch looks at you like that one more time I'm going to slap the shit out of her," Nika said sharply.

"Now you bugging, just chill the fuck out, it's not even that serious," Pop said, trying to defuse the situation before it got out of hand.

"It is that serious, because if it was reversed you would be acting a damn fool and you know it," Nika said cutting her eyes at him.

"Not true at all," he countered smoothly.

"I glad you think everything is so funny," Nika said, nodding her head.

"Babes, I'm not even laughing," he pleaded.

"Okay, y'all enjoy the meal and if there's anything I can get for you just holla, and I do mean anything!" the waitress said, making sure she dragged out the word.

"Get the fuck up out of here!" Nika said as she tossed her drink in the waitress's face.

"Bitch, you must be crazy," the waitress barked as she began to take off her earrings. Before the waitress could retaliate another male waiter had come and grabbed her.

"Bitch, you lucky he's holding me back," the waitress said, desperately try to get loose.

"You better hold that bitch back if you care about her," Nika said, removing a small razor blade from her purse.

"Come on, come on, it's time to go 'cause you don't know how to act," Pop said escorting his woman out of the restaurant. "Baby, you overreacted back there, that lady was just doing her job."

"Yeah, and I was just doing my job, too," Nika shot back, giving Pop a look that could kill.

Instead of engaging in an argument, Pop just remained silent 'cause he knew if the tables had been turned he would have reacted the same way. For the whole walk to the car Pop was quiet as a mouse—the only thing on his mind was how good the makeup sex was going to be.

"Damn, baby, how long you going to be mad for?" Pop asked with a smirk on his face.

"I'm glad you think everything is so funny," Nika said as her and Pop continued to walk to the car.

"Baby, I'm sorry," he said as he hugged her in the middle of the street.

Meanwhile, across the street, Tito sat in the passenger seat of the stolen Acura while his main flunky sat in the driver's seat.

"You sure this the restaurant they in?" Tito asked, running out of patience.

"Yeah, my man just called me and said he saw Pop go up in there with some chick," the Mack answered.

"How reliable is your source?" Tito asked, getting frustrated.

"There that nigga go, right there," the Mack said, pointing at Pop and Nika exiting the restaurant. Once Tito spotted Pop his eyes quickly got as big as peppermint balls. He swiftly pulled his P89 from his waistband and cocked it back.

"You want me to pull up or you wanna take him on foot?" the Mack asked with his .45 sitting on his lap.

"Nah, I'm taking this one on foot. I need him to see my face," Tito said as he slowly slid out of the passenger seat of the Acura. "I want you to pull up down the block and walk down just in case that bitch-ass nigga try to run," Tito ordered as he pulled the strings down on his hoodie while he proceeded to cross the street.

"I'ma make it up to you when we get home," Pop said as he draped his arm around Nika's neck. "Plus you know I only got eyes for you," he told her.

"I bet you tell all the ladies that," Nika said as she spun

around so she could come out of Pop's arms. When she spun around she saw a hooded man carrying something shiny in his hand.

"Baby, watch out!" Nika screamed as she tried to pull Pop into the street and out of the gunman's line of fire.

"Fuck you doing?" Pop said, confused. By the time he realized what was going on he felt something hot and powerful pierce through his shoulder. The impact from the bullet caused Pop to spin around and fall on top of the hood of a parked car. Nika quickly dragged him off the hood of the car onto the concrete as the next two bullets left big dents on the hood of the car and sent other car alarms off.

Once Pop felt the warm blood running down his arm he knew exactly what time it was. "Yo, get down," he yelled as he pulled out his 9 mm, aimed it up at the sky, and let off two shots.

Pow, pow!

Those two shots were just to keep Tito at bay and to give Pop a second to get his thoughts together. "Come on let's go!" Pop said as he and Nika ran at a low, hunched-down squat as they ran down the line of parked cars. Pop's heart was beating a thousand miles per second, not 'cause he was scared but because he didn't want anything to happen to Nika 'cause of him. Once Pop reached the end of the block he thought he was out of harm's way until he saw another hooded man holding something in his hand. Pop quickly raised his 9 mm and sent three shots in the man's direction.

The flunky managed to dodge all the bullets and returned four shots of his own. One of the bullets exploded in a car window right above Nika's head, causing shattered glass to rain down on top of her head. Straight ahead the flunky contin-ued popping shots the whole time, still walking forward. Not knowing what else to do, Pop quickly sprang up from behind the parked car, firing. One shot found a home in Tito's thigh. The impact from the shot caused Tito to stumble backward and he crashed into a parked car, not before letting off a shot of his own. The bullet grazed Pop's neck, causing him to drop down to one knee.

Once the flunky saw Pop drop to a knee he was about to go in for the kill, until he heard the sound of more than one siren.

"Fuck!" the flunky huffed as he ran over to Tito's aid. "Come on we gotta get the fuck out of here!" he yelled as he placed Tito's arm around his neck and help escort him back to the stolen Acura.

"Oh my God, baby, are you okay?" Nika asked as she picked Pop's 9 mm up from the ground and stuck it in her bag before the cops arrived.

"You all right?" Pop asked weakly.

"Yeah, I'm fine just got some glass stuck in my foot," she answered with a smile.

"You too good to me," Pop said as he watched a swarm of cop cars pull up, followed by an ambulance.

"Yo, we going to have to come back on this nigga twice as hard, but we have to be smart at the same time," Fresh said, speaking to a roomful of his soldiers. "Any suggestions on how we can get rid of this cocksucker Tito without attracting too much attention?" Fresh asked, leaning back in his chair.

"There's no way you can kill a loud nigga quiet," Rusty stated, taking a pause. "We just going to have to go out and find this mu'fucka old-school style."

"Yeah, I think you right," Fresh agreed. "Fuck it, we going

old school on this mu'fucka. Rusty, I want you to pay his moms a little visit, don't hurt her too bad, just make sure she delivers our message, the rest of y'all niggas hit them streets, and try to find that clown," Fresh ordered, ending the meeting.

Once everybody was gone Rusty locked the door, before he began to talk. "We going to have to make a strong statement 'cause you know the streets is talking, this mu'fucka Tito running around taking over niggas' blocks, and doing a whole bunch of other shit, in the streets he's looking like Mr. Untouchable."

"Yeah, that's why I want you to pay his moms a visit," Fresh said quickly. "Like I told you, make sure she delivers our message to him," he said, winking at Rusty.

"Say no more, I'm going to get on that right now," Rusty said as he made his exit.

Pop sat laid up in the hospital waiting for his nurse to bring him his discharge papers. "Damn, this shit is taking forever."

"Have patience, baby," Nika said, sitting right by Pop's side.

"As soon as I get out the first person I'm going to see is Tito," he said with anger in his voice.

"No, baby, that shit is over with," Nika told him.

"What if you would of got shot the other night?"

"But I didn't get shot, baby," Nika pointed out. "The shit is over with so let's just move on with our lives. You need to just be happy you are still alive."

"I been trying to let it go but I just can't," Pop said, shaking his head. "I didn't start this beef, but I'm definitely going to finish it."

Nika just shook her head. "You got the world in your hands and you about to throw it all away for what? Some stupid-ass jail nigga that won't make it to live past next year. You smarter then that, Pop."

"This nigga got me laying up in a hospital bed and you want me to just let it go?"

"Pop!" Nika said, grabbing his face. "Let it go, baby, it's not worth it. He shot you and you shot him back that's it it's over with."

"You know what, baby?" Pop began. "You are absolutely right, this shit is not even worth it." Just as he was about to give Nika a kiss, the Chinese detective busted in his room.

"Can we help you?" Nika asked with an attitude.

"Just can't stay out of trouble can you?" The detective said, shaking his head.

"What do you want?" Nika asked in a uninterested tone.

"I just need to ask your boyfriend a few questions," the Chinese detective said, turning to face Pop. "Who shot you?"

"A yo, my man," Pop huffed. "I done already told the other cop what happened earlier already."

"Well, now you can tell me," the detective said as he pulled out his pen and pad.

"Listen, just like I told your friend, we was at a restaurant, I had a few drinks. As soon as we came out the restaurant somebody was having a shoot-out and we got caught up in the middle of it," Pop lied effortlessly.

"Did you happen to see one of the shooter's faces?" the detective asked.

"Nah, the shit happened mad fast," Pop told him.

"I know you lying, you little shit," the Chinese detective said, getting all up in Pop's face. "You play in fire long enough and you going to get burned," he said as he turned on his heels and stormed out of the room.

"And stay out, mu'fucka!" Pop yelled loud enough so that

the detective could hear him. "I can't stand them fuckin' pigs," he said as him and Nika busted out laughing.

Once out of the hospital Nika helped Pop inside the car.

"I'm done with all this shit," Pop said as he leaned back and turned up the new Fabolous CD *Loso's Way*. "I'm just going to get this money until we be out."

"It's about time," Nika said, smiling, as she pulled out into traffic. "That street shit ain't how it used to be anyway, might as well get out while you can and count your blessings."

For the rest of the ride home Pop just sat deep in his own thoughts as he enjoyed the ride.

"Damn!" Tito winced in pain. "Take it easy"

"Stop being a pussy," Maria joked as she stitched up Tito's leg. Maria and Tito had been together since high school. The two fought all the time, but it was always out of love. They would always threaten to leave one another, but the truth was neither one of them was going anywhere.

"Stop being a pussy?" Tito repeated. "Fuck you, this shit hurts. Let me shoot you in your leg and see if you like how it feels."

"First of all, ain't no young nigga or bitch going to pop me and still be walking around," Maria said as she finished stitching her man up. "You let that young boy get the drop on you, you must be getting old, papi," she joked.

"Fuck you mean getting old?" Tito asked as he limped over to the kitchen where Maria stood.

"Don't act like that, papi, you know I was just joking." Maria tried to laugh it off and downplay the situation.

"It look like I'm fuckin' joking right now?" Tito asked as he turned and smacked the shit out of Maria. The impact from the slap caused her to stumble back against the counter.

"Baby, I was just joking," Maria said, holding the side of her face as she saw Tito still coming toward her.

"Shut the fuck up!" he snarled as he swung five hard blows that hit Maria in her face and on the top of her head. "Now laugh at that shit!" he said as he limped into the back room. Maria lay on the floor crying, feeling stupid. She knew how Tito was and how he got down. And she knew she should have just kept her mouth shut.

After forty-five minutes of wild sex Pop was ready to go straight to sleep, but his ringing cell phone caught his attention. When he looked at the caller ID he saw Fresh's name flashing across the screen. Immediately, Pop pressed the no button on his phone and placed it on the dresser.

Pop didn't bother to answer his phone; he knew Fresh was only calling for two reasons: one, to kill somebody, and two, to kill somebody. Pop was tired of living like that. If Fresh wanted him he would just have to wait until tomorrow.

"Two more weeks, and I'm gone," Pop said to himself as he placed Nika in his arms and fell asleep.

The next morning Pop woke up to the sound of his ringing cell phone.

"Who the fuck is that calling so fuckin' early," Nika growled, mad that the phone had interrupted her beauty sleep.

When Pop looked at the caller ID he saw Fresh's name flashing across the screen again.

"Yoooo," Pop answered, still half asleep.

"Where the fuck you been at all night? I been trying to contact you," Fresh barked into the receiver angrily.

"Yeah, I was out late last night and my battery died on my jack," Pop lied.

"Yo, you know where the new spot is at, right?" Fresh asked.

"Yeah, I know where it's at," Pop answered, looking at his wristwatch.

"Good, get over here 'cause I need to holla at you," Fresh said, hanging up in Pop's ear.

"This mu'fucka starting to get out of control," Pop said to himself, still looking at the phone.

"Baby, I'll be right back, I have to go take care of something," he stated, hopping out of the bed.

"You want me to make you some breakfast before you go?" Nika asked, sitting up.

"Nah, I'm not hungry," Pop answered as he planted a kiss on his girl's lips, then headed toward the door.

"Okay be careful out there," Nika said, tossing the covers back over her head.

"So what's so important that it couldn't wait until the afternoon?" Pop asked as soon as he stepped through the door.

"What the fuck has been going on with you? You haven't been yourself lately, seems like something is bothering you," Fresh said, pouring himself a drink.

"Nah, everything is cool, I just been a little busy with a few other things, you dig?" Pop said.

"You know if something is wrong you can come talk to me, right?"

"Yeah, I know," Pop answered quickly.

"The real reason I called you down here was because I wanted to know did you know where Melissa was," Fresh asked.

"Nah, I haven't seen her in a long time," Pop replied.

"How long is a long time?" Fresh asked suspiciously.

"Let me think," Pop said, searching his memory. "The last time I saw her was in the parking lot at the supermarket if I'm not mistaken," he lied with a straight face.

"Listen, Pop, I know you and her were involved with each other, so if you know where she's hiding please let me know, 'cause if I find out you're hiding her it's not going to be a pretty scene," Fresh warned.

"Listen, B. I just told you I don't know where the fuck she's at, right?" Pop said, raising his voice.

"Listen, you watch your tone in my presence," Fresh said, pointing his finger at him.

"Ever since I started dealing with you have I lied to you? So why the fuck would I start now?"

"Pop, I just want to make sure you do the right thing, I got a lot to lose if this shit blows up in my face," Fresh said, covering all of his bases.

"I feel you, but this what I'm going to do: I'm going to personally hunt this bitch down, and kill her myself just for you." Pop stated plainly.

"Good looking, I appreciate it," Fresh said, giving Pop a pound.

"Matter of fact, I'm going to get on that right now," Pop said as he stood up and made his exit.

"Fuck!" Pop screamed loudly as he hopped in his Benz.

Pop knew he had fucked up. Instead of Melissa going out of town he had convinced her to live in a hotel with him for a while until they came up with a plan. It was hard for Pop to get away from Melissa. When he would go home with Nika, he would tell Melissa he was going to take care of some business, but he knew it would only be a matter of time before the plan went sour and he got busted.

Pop quickly pulled out his cell phone and dialed Melissa's number.

"Hello?" she answered in a frail voice.

"What you doing?"

"Waiting for you to come back," Melissa said, as her voice changed into a whining tone.

"Listen, I don't want you to leave that hotel room, okay?"

"Why what's wrong?" Melissa asked with her voice full of panic.

"Nothing, just do what I tell you," he told her.

"Pop, if something is wrong I think you should tell me," Melissa said pushing the issue.

"Listen, I don't have time to explain, just do what I tell you," Pop said in a firm tone.

"Pop, what am I suppose to eat? 'cause ain't shit in this mu'fucka to eat," Melissa whined.

"Just be cool for a minute, I'm going to bring you some groceries over there a'ight?"

"Okay, just hurry up 'cause I'm starving," Melissa said, pouting like a child.

"Okay, I'll be over there in about an hour," he said, ending the conversation.

Melissa stood in the hotel room drying off her wet body. She knew that something was wrong, but she just couldn't figure out what.

Melissa stood in front of the full-length mirror, applying lotion on her beautiful skin, when she heard a key unlock the front door. "Hey, baby what's up?" she asked, standing in the middle of the room naked as she watched Pop come through the door with both of his hands full with groceries.

"What's up, babes? I brought some DVDs for us to watch since you sounded so bored."

"I'm not bored, I just missed you," Melissa said, wrapping her arms around Pop's neck as she hugged him.

"How much you missed me?" he asked, cuffing both of Melissa's ass cheeks in the palm of his hands.

"I can show you better than I can tell you," Melissa said in her heavy accent as she dropped down to her knees. As soon as Pop felt Melissa tugging at his belt buckle his manhood immediately rose and was ready for action. He watched as Melissa slowly licked on the head of his dick like it was an ice cream cone. Pop loved how wet Melissa's mouth was, along with all the sexy sounds that she made.

"I want you to fuck my mouth, papi," Melissa begged, holding Pop's dick in a two-handed grip. Pop immediately grabbed the back of Melissa's head and began fuckin' her mouth like it was a pussy. He fucked her mouth so good that juices and saliva began to run from the corner of her mouth and down her chin. When Pop felt his orgasm building up he quickly took a step back.

"Turn around," he demanded as he watched Melissa turn around and bend over on the counter. Melissa gasped when she felt Pop inside of her; it was as if his dick and her pussy were the perfect match. Pop wanted to take his time but the way Melissa was looking he knew it wouldn't be a long night. He started off with slow, deep strokes, making sure that Melissa felt every inch of him as he spread both of her ass cheeks apart watching himself go in and out of her love box.

"Mmm . . . papi," Melissa moaned as she began to throw her ass back, causing a clapping sound to form as her ass bounced off Pop's torso. Pop pulled Melissa's hair and turned her head to the side so he could see her face while he fucked the shit out of her. Seconds later he came all over her ass cheeks.

"Oh my God, *papi* I love my dick," Melissa said, out of breath as she walked to the bathroom to clean herself off.

Twenty minutes later she found herself in the kitchen cooking dinner. "So, baby, what's the deal about me staying in this hotel all day?" Melissa asked, seasoning the chicken in front of her.

"Nothing, I just don't really want you to be out in the streets until I find out who killed Amanda, "cause you never know, you might be next on the list," Pop said flatly. "I just don't want to see anything bad happen to you."

"I understand, baby," Melissa responded.

In all reality Pop knew Fresh had people out on the streets looking for Melissa and Tito right now. All Pop wanted to do was leave the state without anybody close to him getting hurt, and that's just what he planned on doing. He was running out of time and he felt it in his heart. He knew he could be the next one to end up dead.

Week Three

"I heard Fresh got a couple of dollars on your head," Bamboo said, letting out a light chuckle. "So how you going to play it?"

"Listen if this mu'fucka want a war then that's just what the fuck he going to get, "cause I ain't hiding," Tito said as him and Bamboo traded duffel bags.

"I see you got yourself a little entourage," Bamboo said, noticing the four men following Tito around.

"Come on, B. You know I'm still on parole, I can't always be the shooter," Tito said, smirking.

"Where you headed?" Bamboo asked with a smile on his face.

"To break this down," Tito said, nodding to the duffel bag. "Why, what's up?" he asked, noticing the smile that rested on Bamboo's face.

"Word on the streets is Fresh and your Friend Rusty supposed to be having a big cookout at some park downtown."

"Fuck outta here," Tito said in disbelief. "Who told you that shit?"

"Some chick that I deal with, she knows some chick that messes with Rusty," Bamboo answered.

"What time that shit supposed to be going down?" Tito asked with a thirsty look in his eyes.

Bamboo flipped his arm so he could look at his watch. "Right now," he said with a smile.

"Fuck that, I'm about to go crash that shit," Tito said. "You coming?"

"What you think, I'ma stay here and just let you have all the fun? Fuck outta here," Bamboo said as he, Tito, and Tito's entourage made their exit.

"Damn, it's hot as fuck out here," Rusty complained, wiping the sweat from his forehead with a rag. "I ain't never seen this many freeloader in my life."

"It's all about giving back," Fresh laughed as he saw Vanessa walking in his direction.

"Hey, daddy, what's up?" Vanessa said as she kissed Fresh on the lips.

"Damn, baby, it's about time you got here," Fresh said playfully as he palmed her ass. "I thought you got lost for a second."

"Shit, it took me like thirty minutes to find a place to park," Vanessa said, smiling.

"It's enough niggas out here to make a Tarzan movie," Rusty said as the three busted out laughing.

"You better go get you a plate before it's all gone" Fresh said.

"Yeah, I think I'ma go do that," Vanessa said as she walked over toward the grill.

"Loosen up and enjoy yourself," Fresh said, throwing two phantom punches at Rusty.

"I'm good," Rusty said, bobbing his head to the music. Everybody at the cookout was enjoying themselves and having a good time. Vanessa stood over in the shade sipping on some bottle. Lil Wayne's new song, "Always Strapped," came blasting through the speakers, getting everybody hype.

"Damn, baby, you over here looking all lonely and shit," Derrick said, approaching Vanessa. Derrick was a petty hustler from around the way who thought he was a player, but really he wasn't about nothing. "Looks like you can use some company," he said, draping his arm around her neck.

"Yo, my man," Vanessa said, removing Derrick's arm from around her neck. "It's mad hot out here; I'ma need you to back up just a taste."

"Don't act like that, ma, I was just coming over to keep you company 'cause you was over here looking all lonely and shit," Derrick said, grabbing her hand.

"That was nice, but I'm good," Vanessa said, still trying to be polite.

"Come dance with me," Derrick said, pulling Vanessa closer to him.

"Maybe later," she said, pulling her hand back.

"But I'm saying, though," Derrick said seductively, getting

all up in Vanessa's face. "A nigga can't get a dance?" he said, sliding his hand on Vanessa's ass.

"Nigga, don't fuckin' touch my ass," Vanessa barked. "Fuck is wrong with you."

"Bitch, shut the fuck up!" Derrick said, debating on whether he should smack the shit out of her.

"Make me, mu'fucka!" Vanessa countered.

Fresh and Rusty stood over on the other side of the park dissing some corny nigga, when Rusty peeped what was going on, on the other side of the park.

"Yo, fam, ain't that Vanessa over there?" Rusty said, pointing over to where Derrick stood, looking like he was about to hit her.

Fresh pulled his shades down so he could get a better look. "Who that, Derrick?"

"Yup," Rusty answered, quickly instigating. Once Rusty saw Fresh head over in that direction, he and a few of the goons quickly followed his lead.

"Whack-ass bitch" Derrick said, sipping from his cup of Henny.

"If I'm so wack why is you sweating me?" Vanessa asked with her face screwed up. "Bum-ass nigga."

"Sweating you?" Derrick said with a confused look on his face. "You can't be serious. You out here looking like a fiend with a fat ass. Get the fuck outta here!"

"Your mother look like a fiend," Vanessa shot back. Those last words really hit Derrick's heart because his mother was really on drugs.

"What?" Derrick said, stepping toward Vanessa.

"You heard me," she said, taking a step back.

Just as Derrick was about to swing he a felt punch to the side of his head. Before he knew what was going on he felt punches coming from all angles. Once Derrick fell to the ground Fresh stomped his head into the ground until Rusty and the rest of the crew had to pull him off of.

"Yo, chill, you gon' fuck around and kill this nigga by accident," Rusty said, holding Fresh back. Once the scuffle was over Remy Martin's song, "Conceited," came blasting from the speakers and everybody continued on partying like a man didn't just get beat half to death.

"Look at these clowns," Bamboo said, sitting in the driver's seat of the van.

"I'm about to dump on these niggas," Tito said, ready to get it poppin'.

"Hold up while I get a little closer," Bamboo said, slowly cruising past.

"Look at these faggots," Tito said as he watched Fresh and his crew jump Derrick. "Man, fuck all this dump," he said as he stuck his Mac 11 out the window and let it spit. Once Tito let that thing off his flunkies snatched open the side door on the van and began popping shots as well.

"You a'ight?" Rusty asked, handing Fresh a drink.

"Yeah, I'm good," Fresh replied, sipping on his drink. "I can't never just chill and enjoy myself."

Just as Rusty was about reply a series of gunshots rang out. Immediately everybody got low and began running for cover.

Fresh quickly pulled his .45 and began returning fire as he backed away.

Rusty took cover behind a tree as he returned fire. Once Tito ran out of bullets Bamboo put the pedal to the metal.

"That's what I'm talking about," Tito yelled once they were on the highway. "I hit like twenty of them niggas," he boasted.

Once all the shots finished ringing out Fresh quickly ran over to where Vanessa stood. "You a'ight?"

"Yeah, I'm fine I just skinned my knee when I heard the gunshots," Vanessa said as she and Fresh headed to their car along with everybody before the cops arrived.

"How much is this?" Pop asked.

"That's five stacks right there," Jason answered, handing Pop the stack of money.

"Yo, grab that work from out of that milk crate for me," Pop said as he exited the basement of the bodega.

Once he stepped outside Pop saw fiends coming left and right. "Another day, another dollar," he said to himself, taking a breath of fresh air.

"Yo, I'll be right back I'm about to go hand out these packs real quick," Jason said as he went to handle his business.

As Pop stood on the block, he wondered what would be the better choice: to tell Fresh he wanted out or should he not say anything, and just be out?

Pop's thoughts were rudely interrupted when he noticed five cars pull up back-to-back right across the street from him. "What the fuck is this?" he asked himself as he watched at least fifteen guys hop out the vehicles posting up directly across the street.

"Who the fuck are these niggas?" Jason asked, reappearing on the scene.

"I don't know but we about to find out I'm guessing," Pop responded. Two minutes later Pop saw Tito cruise by slowly in his Porsche with an evil smirk on his face.

"Yo, J, go strap up!" Pop ordered.

"Say no more," Jason said as he disappeared inside of the bodega. "Yo, Mannie pass me that toaster," he said to the store owner. Without hesitation Mannie handed Jason a .40-caliber from behind the counter.

"Yo, shorty, du-wop," Pop called out to one of his young workers. "Yo, take this Benz and pull around to the back of the bodega," Pop said, tossing his worker the keys to his Benz.

"You want me to clear this shit out?" Jason asked, reappearing on the scene clutching the .40-caliber.

"Yeah, clear this shit the fuck out," Pop ordered as he headed for the bodega. Immediately Jason raised the .40 cal, and let it pop. *Bak, bak, bak, bak, bak!*

The fifteen men quickly scrambled to hop back in their vehicles they came in. Unfortunately, only fourteen of the men made it off the block alive.

Once Jason cleared out the block he quickly ran inside the bodega. "Here, take this, I'm out," he said, handing Mannie back the .40-caliber as he slid out the back door right into the passenger's seat of the awaiting Benz.

"Clockwork," Pop chuckled as he stepped on the gas.

"Yo, what you wanna do for your birthday?" Tito asked as he stopped at the red light.

"Nothing really, I just want to spend the night with you," Maria replied.

"Damn, you don't want to do nothing?" Tito asked, clearly disappointed.

"I just want to spend the night with you only, just you and me," Maria whined as she slid her fingers in between his.

"We can do that," Tito sighed. "My man just text me, he over at this lounge downtown. I told him to check it out for me, I was thinking about buying it." He paused. "Let's swing down there for about twenty minutes then I promise we can leave, and spend the rest of the night together," he said waiting for her response.

"Twenty minutes and that's it," Maria said flatly.

Twenty-five minutes later, Tito parked across the street from the lounge.

"Twenty minutes," Maria said reminding her man so he knew she was serious. As soon as the couple stepped inside the lounge it was packed. The music was blasting and people were all around doing their own thing. Tito quickly made his way over to the bar to where a few of his Spanish goons stood.

"What you think of the place?" Tito asked, handing Maria a cup of Grey Goose and pineapple juice—her favorite.

"I like it," she answered looking at the potential the place had. She knew Tito was a hustler and that he could make something out of nothing, so whatever her man had in mind she was behind him a hundred percent.

"I get this popping, then I won't have to be out in the streets too tough," Tito lied, trying to get Maria to see things his way.

"I like this, plus it's in a good location," she added, looking around.

"I got big plans for this place," Tito said, rubbing his hands together. "Let me talk to my man for five minutes, then we gon' be out."

"Okay, baby," she said as she helped herself to a seat on the empty bar stool. She sat on the bar stool, bobbing her head to the music, when she noticed Rusty enter the lounge followed by men. As soon as she Rusty she knew some shit was about to go down. Maria looked over at Tito and saw that crazy look in his eyes.

"Yo, Tony," Tito yelled, calling over the big bouncer. "You see those three niggas that just walked in?"

"Yeah, what about them?" Tony asked, looking over at the three men.

"Do me a favor, go ask your partner did he pat those three men down over there," Tito said, slipping a fifty-dollar bill in Tony's hand.

Tito headed over to the bar as he watched Tony go over and talk to the other bouncer. "Yo, let me get a bottle of champagne," Tito yelled over the counter to the bartender.

"Yeah, they clean," Tony said, returning to the bar.

"A'ight, cool," Tito said as he noticed Rusty and his two soldiers coming over to the bar. From the look on Rusty's face Tito could tell that the man was coming toward the bar for some action.

"Hey," Tony said, placing his paw on Rusty's chest. "Don't come in here with all that."

Rusty quickly slapped the big man's hand away and stole on him. As Tony went stumbling backward, Tito viciously busted the champagne bottle over Rusty's head. Once Rusty hit the floor one of the men he came in with punched Tito in the face, then all hell broke loose. Since the majority of the people in the lounge were Spanish, the once-even fight turned into a one-sided battle. People who didn't even have nothing to do with the situation took turns stomping on Rusty and the two men he came in with. After about ten minutes of beating and pounding on the three men, Tony and the rest of the bouncers dragged Rusty and the two men he came in with out back into the alley like they were trash.

"Stupid mu'fucka!" Tito growled as he spit right on Rusty's face. "Fuck you think this shit is a game," he said out loud as he searched through Rusty's pockets, stripping him of all his jewelry and money. "Tell that bitch Fresh he's next," Tito said as he gave Rusty one last kick.

"Who?" Fresh yelled into the phone. "Fuck that, get there now," he said, hanging up the phone. Fresh stood up from his desk and removed his .45 from the small of his back and checked the magazine.

"Fuck that I ain't got time for all this waiting shit," he said, looking over at Tim, who was a new goon that Rusty had just hired the other day. "Yo, strap up you coming with me."

"What's wrong?" Tim asked nervously as he grabbed his baby Uzi and stuck a fresh magazine in the base.

"I just got word Rusty in the hospital," Fresh said with a disgusted look on his face. "That mu'fucka, Tito," he huffed as he slid in the passenger seat of the minivan.

"Where we headed?" Tim asked as he started up the van and pulled out into traffic.

"First, we going to swing by the lounge where they found Rusty and light that shit the fuck up," Fresh said in a calm tone as he sat back and threw on his black shades.

Twenty minutes later, Tim pulled up across the street from the lounge. "This the lounge right here?" he asked.

"Yeah, pass me that Uzi," Fresh said, tossing his hood on his head. "Swing this bitch around," he said, rolling down his window.

In front of the lounge stood Tony and few other bouncers standing around talking shit.

"What's poppin'?" Fresh said with a smile. The last thing Tony saw was his reflection in Fresh's shades before his body got riddled and rocked. Fresh squeezed the trigger until he ran out of bullets. The front of the lounge was filled with holes and shattered glass everywhere.

Once Tim heard the Uzi stop spitting, he immediately gunned the engine, fleeing the scene.

"Where we headed now?" Tim asked, driving like a madman.

"Slow this mu'fucka down," Fresh said, reloading the Uzi. "We going to Tito's first cousin's crib," he said as he punched her address in the navigational system.

"Which house?" Tim asked, slowly cruising down the block.

"The third house on the right," Fresh answered, pointing to the house.

"You need me to get out?" Tim asked as he pulled up in the driveway.

"Nah, just keep this bitch running," Fresh said as he slid out the passenger seat and headed toward the front door of the house. Once in front of the door he knocked with the barrel of his .45.

Jasmine opened the door with a big smile on her face. "Hey, Fresh," she said, sliding in his arms for a hug. "Where you been, I haven't seen you around in a while," she said, stepping to the side so he could come in.

"My bad, I just been mad busy," Fresh replied. "Is Tito here? I need to holla at him for a second."

"Nah, I haven't seen him in a while either," Jasmine said, walking over to the kitchen. "You want something to drink?"

"No, thank you," Fresh politely declined. He felt bad on the inside because he really liked Jasmine. Throughout the years she was always there when the team needed her. Whether it was holding drugs in her house, taking trips out of town, setting someone up, whatever it was, she was always down.

"Why you got on that hoodie and those dark shades?" Jasmine asked with a smile. Her smile quickly faded away when she saw the .45 in Fresh's hand.

"No, no don't do this Fresh," she pleaded as she backed up. "Whatever is going on with you and Tito has nothing to do with me," she cried as her back hit the counter. She quickly reached over and grabbed a knife from off the dish rack. "Fresh, please don't do this," she begged as tears rolled down her face.

"Put that knife down," Fresh said in a calm tone.

"Please don't do this," Jasmine begged as she dropped the knife and dropped down to her knees. "Please, Fresh," she continued to beg.

Fresh slowly walked over to Jasmine and he grabbed a handful of her hair with one hand as he struck her repeatedly in her exposed face with the gun until she was no longer recognizable. Once Fresh finished beating the woman he roughly tossed her to the floor and aimed his .45 at Jasmine's head.

"Please, Fresh, don't do this," she begged for her life. Fresh had his gun trained on Jasmine's head, but he just couldn't pull the trigger for some reason. Jasmine really didn't have nothing to do with nothing, but Fresh had to send a message to Tito.

"I'm sorry," Fresh whispered as he turned around and exited the house.

"Thank you, Fresh!" she yelled as she watched his departing back exit her home. Jasmine lay on the floor thanking God that Fresh didn't kill her. She knew for a fact that if she had been anyone else she would be a dead woman right now.

"Everything went okay in there?" Tim asked, noticing he didn't hear no gunshots go off inside the house.

"Yeah, everything is good," Fresh answered quickly. "Take me home, I need to get some rest," he told him.

"No problem," Tim said, doing as he was told. He could tell something was wrong with Fresh, but he played it cool and decided to just mind his business.

"This shit done got personal," Tito said, filling his cup up to the top with straight Hennessy.

"How you wanna play it?" Bamboo asked, playing with his .357

"Somebody gon' have to die," Tito said simply. "I'm tired of playing with these clowns."

"Fuck it, I got my hit squad already on standby, just give me the word," Bamboo said.

"Nah, fuck that I gotta do this shit myself," Tito said, looking at his P89. Fresh was the one who taught him everything he knew. So he knew the shit wouldn't end until one of them got killed.

"I got a plan," Bamboo said, loading his .357. "You used to work for Fresh, right?"

"Yeah, and?"

"Yeah, and that means you know where the nigga's stash spots is at, right?" Bamboo asked greedily.

"He switches them shits up every week," Tito said. "But I do know where all his cookup spots is at."

"Damn, why you ain't been said nothing about this?" Bamboo said excitedly.

"I forgot all about that shit," Tito chuckled. "But fuck all that, I want Fresh."

"Well, we both know he's too much of a pussy to play the streets so I guess we going to have to smoke him out," Bamboo stated plainly.

"Fuck it, let the games begin."

***

Fresh cruised down the street in his Benz listening to a Stack Bundles mix tape, when out of the blue he noticed flashing lights in his rearview mirror. "Shit!" he cursed loudly as he pulled over to the side of the road. He quickly slipped his .45 in the stash box on his dashboard. He also put out the blunt he'd been smoking. "Ain't this about a bitch," Fresh said to himself as he looked in his rearview mirror and saw three more cars pull up behind him.

"Hands on the steering wheel," a uniform cop yelled, flashing the light from his flashlight in Fresh's face while the other officers surrounded the car.

Fresh sighed loudly as he did what he was told. The officer then roughly grabbed him from out of the car and tossed him on the floor and cuffed him.

"What did I do!" Fresh yelled as he felt the officers searching through his pockets, while the rest of the officers searched his car. "I didn't even do nothing!" Fresh yelled as he struggled to not let them put him in the back of the squad car. Once the officers saw Fresh resisting arrest they immediately began swinging their night sticks at his legs until he hit the ground.

"You had to do things the hard way," the head officer said as dragged Fresh into the back of the squad car and took him down to the station.

Rusty parked the Ford Explorer directly in front of the house that he was headed for. Before Rusty reached the front door he made sure he threw his gloves on along with his hoodie, as he proceeded to kick in the front door. Tito's mother almost shitted on herself when she saw her front door fly open. Immediately Rusty back-slapped Tito's mot-her with the .45, sending her crashing to the kitchen floor. Before he could strike her again, he noticed Tito's father come running into the living room.

Before the elderly man knew what was going on two shots to both of his kneecaps sent him straight on his back. Once Tito's mother heard the loud gunshots ring out she immediately grabbed her heart and began gasping for air. Rusty looked on for about thirty seconds until the woman stopped moving. "Weak-ass bitch," he said, shrugging his shoulders. He then proceeded to search the entire house, hoping Tito had a safe or a stash somewhere inside the house. As Rusty searched through the house he made sure he tore the place up. He walked over to the nice wall unit and pulled the whole shit down, leaving a big mess. He flipped over all the couches, the mattress, and anything else he could as he continued his search. After about ten minutes of searching Rusty made his way back to the living room and placed the .45 to Tito's father's head.

"I know Tito got a stash in here somewhere now where is it?" Rusty growled.

"Ain't no stash. He never keeps drugs or money here," Tito's father answered, still clutching both of his kneecaps.

"Last time I'm gonna ask you, old man," Rusty stated in an even tone. When the old man didn't answer Rusty began to beat the old man with the .45 until his face looked like tomato soup. That still didn't stop him; he continued to pound on the old man's face, lecturing him the whole time.

"You think it's a fuckin' a game?" Rusty snarled as noticed the old man wasn't moving anymore. A wicked smile appeared on his face as he stood up and admired his work. He took a quick look around, then walked right back out the front door like nothing ever even happened.

***

"Who's the owner of this store?" The Chinese detective asked.

"Who's concerned?" Mannie shot back, obeying one of the street commandments: Always give the police a hard time.

"Who the fuck is asking, shitface?" the Chinese Detective responded.

"I'm sorry, Detective, but I don't speak no English," Mannie stated as he tossed a piece of gum in his mouth.

"I'll be back with a warrant, and when I come back I'm going to tear this place up," the Chinese detective warned. The detective fought to control his temper as he quietly exited the bodega.

Fresh sat in the bullpen, sitting on the hard bench with a thousand thoughts running through his mind. The police told him that he was in jail for assaulting Tito's cousin Jasmine. It didn't matter to Fresh, though, because he knew he would soon be getting bailed out. Sitting in jail wasn't a problem to him. His problem was the police— he couldn't stand them. Inside they were the toughest people in the world, but if you were to ever see them out in the streets it was a different story. Fresh sat in the bullpen waiting to get bailed out when he saw this dirty, rough-looking man walk into the bullpen. Immediately Fresh didn't like the man. The dirty man came in the bullpen sneezing and coughing. "Damn," he snarled as he held one of his nostrils and blew snot out of his nose onto the floor a little bit too close to Fresh.

"Yo, watch that shit," Fresh said with his face screwed up. "Nasty mu'fucka!"

"Fuck you," the dirty man countered. "This a free country last time I checked." The dirty man continued: "You young boys think y'all all that until somebody knock y'all the fuck out."

Fresh hopped up with the quickness and stole on the dirty man, dropping him off impact alone. He then quickly hopped up on top of the man and began raining punches on the man exposed face until the dirty man stopped moving.

Fresh stomped the man's head into the pavement one last time before he left the man alone. He walked back over to his seat and just left the dirty man laid out in the middle of the floor. The rest of the inmates just acted like nothing ever happened and continued on doing whatever it was they were doing.

"*Que hora es?*" Tito asked, trying to find out what time it was.

"It's 5:45 P.M." Maria answered.

Maria loved being Tito's main girl; she had a pretty face and a nice body. Her good looks fooled a lot of people . . . this Dominican was far from an angel. Maria grew up in the street, plus being involved with Tito for so long, drama was a small thing to her.

"What the fuck is taking your fat-ass sister so long?" Tito asked, getting upset.

"Shut up, papi," Maria said from the passenger seat.

"There her fat ass go right there," Tito said, pointing at the two-hundred-and-fifty-pound woman.

"Sorry I'm late," Amber said as the whole car got lower once she got inside.

"Now where the fuck are we going?" Tito asked with an attitude. He hated helping Maria's sister; every week it was something new with her.

"I told you we going to the supermarket 'cause Amber don't have any food for her kids," Maria said rolling her eyes.

"She probably ate it all," Tito mumbled as he pulled into the supermarket parking lot.

Inside the supermarket Nika stood on the long-ass line waiting to pay for her groceries. All she could think about was leaving to go to Miami. She had never been outside of New York and was so looking forward to the move. But more importantly she was excited for Pop. She knew he badly needed a change of scenery. Just by the way he'd been acting lately she could tell something was bothering him, but she knew he would never just come out and tell her, and she didn't ask because she didn't want to be a nag so instead, she just left the situation alone and just continued to count down the days until it was time for the two to leave. Nika stepped out of the supermarket and headed straight for her car.

"Get the fuck out of here," Tito said out loud as he spotted Nika coming out of the supermarket carrying more bags then she could handle.

"What's wrong, baby?" Maria asked curiously.

"That bitch right there slapped me the other day because I didn't want to talk to her," Tito lied.

"Who?" Maria blurted out.

"Shorty right there with the fucked-up weave," Tito said, pointing. Without hesitation Maria and Amber hopped out the vehicle and ran over to catch up to the woman.

Nika headed to her car when out of nowhere a solid blow caught her in the back of her head. The impact from the blow caused Nika to drop her groceries as she struggled to stay on her feet. Once she regained her balance she quickly threw a wild right hook that connected with Maria's jaw. Nika quickly followed up with a left uppercut as she dragged Maria to the ground by her hair.

Before Nika could get another hit off she saw a bigger woman running at her full speed. She did the best she could to block the blow but the force from the big woman's punch still managed to move Nika's whole body.

Before Nika could swing back, Maria had busted her over the head with a gallon of milk that fell out of her grocery bag. "Fuckin' bitch!" Maria screamed in rage as she and Amber rained blow after blow on Nika's exposed face until it was covered with blood and cuts from the rings the two women wore.

"Hey, that's enough," an innocent bystander shouted as he attempted to break up the fight.

"Yo, my man, mind your fuckin' business," Tito said, placing his P89 to the man's rib cage.

Once the crowd started getting too large Tito figured it was time to be out. "Yo, that's it, we out," Tito said, breaking up the fight. "Tell your punk-ass boyfriend he's next," he said as he kicked Nika in the face before he disappeared through the crowd.

"That's what the fuck I'm talking about," Tito said, watching the scene disappear through his rearview mirror.

"Fuck that, don't nobody be putting they hands on my man," Maria said, trying to fix her hair in the small mirror.

"Yo, here, you going to have to take a cab to another supermarket," Tito said, handing Amber $300 dollars as he dropped her off at her apartment.

"Call me later, girl," Amber said to her sister right before the vehicle pulled off.

"That was good work back there baby," Tito said, kissing Maria on the cheek.

"You know I'll do anything for you, papi," she responded, fiddling with the radio.

"Oh, shit, I forgot I was supposed to do your mother's hair today," she blurted out.

"Well, you can't because we going out tonight," Tito said, stroking Maria's hair.

"That's not right, Tito," she told him.

"Fuck that, do her hair tomorrow," he dismissed.

"But I promised her I would do it today; at least take me over there so I can tell her I'll do it tomorrow," Maria huffed.

"Use your cell phone and just call her," Tito stated with a wave of his hand.

"Tito, stop being lazy and take me over there," Maria demanded.

"You get on my fuckin' nerves," Tito snarled as he made a detour.

"And then he kicked me in my face," Nika said, trying to stop the tears from flowing as she sat on the couch.

"It's going to be okay, baby," Pop said, trying to calm his woman down. "Stop crying, baby, you know I'm going to make that mu'fucka pay for this shit when I catch his ass."

"I know, baby, I did the best I could," Nika sobbed.

"I know, baby, that's why they had to jump you," Pop said, putting an emotional bandage on her ego.

"I'm going to wear that big bitch out if I catch her by myself," Nika said, replaying the whole scene in her head.

"Nah, baby, I'm going to take care of this you just get your shit ready to leave next week," he said as he placed a clip in his 9 mm.

"I'll be back, I'm going to go see if I can catch one of these mu'fuckas slipping," Pop stated flatly as he threw on his hoodie, and headed out the door.

Fresh walked out the bookings with a frown on his face. "Racist mu'fuckas!" he growled as he slid in the passenger seat of the ride that awaited him.

"Fuck took you so long?" Rusty asked as he pulled off.

"Fuckin' pigs had me sitting in there for three extra hours for nothing," Fresh complained. "I had to fuck me a nigga up in there and all that."

"Word?" Rusty laughed. "All in a day's work."

"How did that other thing go?" Fresh asked as he grabbed the blunt from out the ashtray and lit it up.

"A piece of cake," Rusty chuckled. "When I catch that bitch-ass nigga Tito I might just kill him with my bare hands."

"We going to catch him," Fresh said in between puffs. "It's just a matter of time," he said convincingly.

"That mu'fucka better just keep on hiding," Rusty said, still mad that Tito and the other men at the bar had fucked him up.

"Patience, just have some patience," Fresh said, plucking his ashes out the window. "Tito's pride is gonna bring him out of hiding. You just wait and see."

"Well, he need to hurry up because I'm tired of playing games with this clown," Rusty huffed. "Matter of fact, I might just go out riding tonight looking for that clown."

"Shit, if I know Tito the way I think I do I wouldn't be surprised if he'd be out riding looking for us," Fresh said, leaning his seat all the way back.

***

"What the fuck is this?" Tito asked as he saw the always-dark street lit up by the many police cars. Immediately Tito passed his P89 to Maria. She had been through this drill a million times. She quickly tossed the gun in her pocket book like it was not a crime.

"What the fuck is going on here?" Tito asked a police officer as his tinted window came rolling down.

"Sir, just keep on moving, this matter doesn't concern you!" the rednecked officer answered.

"I live here, mu'fucka," Tito yelled as he hopped out of the vehicle and ran toward his mother's house.

"I'm sorry, you can't go any further," another police officer said as he restrained him.

"You are going to have to wait until the detectives finish looking around, sir."

"Well, can you at least tell me what the fuck is going on?" Tito asked the officer.

"It seems like a burglary took place. The man of the house took two shots to his legs and the woman of the house seems to have had a heart attack." Immediately Tito broke down into tears. He already knew what time it was; he knew this was the work of Fresh, because Fresh was the very man who had trained him.

Tito no longer wanted to go inside, instead he grabbed Maria by the wrist and jumped back inside his vehicle, driving away from the house he had once grown up in.

"Are you okay?" Maria asked.

Tito didn't answer, instead he remained silent. The thoughts that were racing through his mind were ones of an insane person. His mother was all he had and now that she was gone there was no telling what he would do.

Chapter Nineteen

Week Four

"Melissa, Melissa!" Pop yelled.

When he didn't get an answer he quickly snatched his 9 mm from his waistband and checked the entire hotel room, making sure no one was inside.

"I told her not to leave this fuckin' room," Pop said to himself, wondering where she could be.

After thirty minutes of waiting he heard a key unlock the top lock on the door, followed by the bottom lock. Melissa strolled in, never noticing Pop sitting there as she came in with her hands full of bags.

"Where the fuck you been?"

"Oh, shit, Pop, you scared the shit out of me, why are you sitting here in the dark?" Melissa said, startled.

"Didn't I tell you not to leave this fuckin' hotel room?" Pop growled.

"Yeah, I know, I just went to Victoria's Secret so I could get me a few new pieces, so I could put on a show for you later," she said naively. She meant well, but her actions were so stupid.

"Why can't you just listen?" he asked smugly.

"Pop I've been stuck in this hotel room for three weeks, three long boring weeks, I don't see why I can't go to the fuckin' store—"

Before Melissa could even finish pleading her case they were both caught off guard when their hotel room door flew open. Pop quickly grabbed his 9 mm from off of the coffee table and aimed it at the gunman. He hesitated to pull the trigger when he saw Rusty standing in front of his cannon.

"Rusty, what the fuck are you doing here?" Pop asked, lowering his gun.

"I was coming to kill this bitch," Rusty answered, pointing at Melissa as he too lowered his weapon.

"Rusty, why are you trying to kill me?" Melissa asked, confused. "If I tell Fresh about this you know he going to hand you your ass," she stated boldly.

"Bitch, Fresh is the one who hired Pop to kill your sister, but he didn't have the balls to do you too that's why I'm here," Rusty said, aiming his .357 at the beautiful woman.

"I didn't have the balls? Nigga what the fuck you think I'm doing here right now? I was just about to smoke this bitch until you came busting up in here," Pop stated sharply. "Now I ain't even going to be able to get no pussy before I kill her!"

"If you want we both could get some pussy," Rusty said, looking at Melissa's nice body with a hungry look in his eyes.

"Nah, I have to do this alone," Pop stated aggressively.

"You got it, Pop, just make sure you leave her in this hotel room so it can make the news, that way Fresh can verify you accomplished your mission."

"Not a problem," Pop responded as he escorted Rusty to the door.

"Holla at me when it's all said and done," Rusty said as he gave Pop a pound then disappeared through the front door. Pop slammed the front door then turned toward Melissa.

"You a real piece of shit you know that?" Melissa snarled as tears ran freely from her eyes.

"Wait, baby, let me explain," Pop pleaded.

"Explain?" Melissa exclaimed loudly. "Ain't shit to explain mu'fucka, you told me you would never hurt me," Melissa whispered as she looked at him in pain.

"And I never will, baby," he pleaded again.

"You never will? You murdered my fuckin' sister and made me get in the trunk with her dead body, then pretended you didn't know anything about it."

"Baby, I was going to tell you," he told her.

With the speed of lighting Melissa slapped Pop across his face twice, then tried to dig his eyes out with her nails.

"Chill the fuck out," Pop yelled as he grabbed her arms and pinned her down on the bed. The whole time she was still kicking her legs and screaming. "Calm the fuck down," Pop yelled. "I'm sorry. I swear I was going to tell you." He paused. "I just couldn't."

"Get off of me now!" Melissa said through clenched teeth. "You ain't no real man, you a pussy."

"I'm sorry," Pop said, letting Melissa up.

"That's it—you just sorry, that's all gon' tell me?"

"What do you want me to do?" Pop asked. He really felt bad for what he had done, but what's done is done.

"Why don't you just shoot me? That's why you here, right? Ain't that what you just told Rusty right? So do what you got to do," Melissa said, removing her shirt and bra.

"Shoot me right in my heart, Pop, go ahead, what you waiting for? You already done ripped it in half, you might as well shoot it out," Melissa said, getting all up in Pop's face. "Don't be a pussy now, you shot my sister."

"Baby, let me explain." He tried to plead his case again, but once again he got cut off.

"Why, Pop? Why did you do it?" Melissa asked as she mel-

ted inside of Pop's arms. "She ain't never did nothing to nobody. All she wanted was to be loved."

"I'm sorry," Pop whispered as he stroked Melissa's curly
hair.

It wasn't much Pop could do but say sorry. The last thing
he wanted was for Melissa to find out like this; if it was up to
him he would have made sure she never found out what really
happened that night but now it was too late.

"So you have to kill me right now don't you?" Melissa asked
in a light whisper.

"You know I wouldn't lay a finger on you," Pop assured her.

"Baby, I didn't want to hurt you but I was in a no-win
situation. Fresh thought your sister was going to tell the cops
everything she knew, and he couldn't let it go down like that.
You know how the game goes."

"So if you don't kill me then what's going to happen to
you?" she asked as her shoulders went up and down from her
sobbing getting worse.

"Let me worry about that," Pop told her. "When that bridge
comes then I'll cross it."

Melissa didn't respond, instead she just studied Pop's face.
She could tell that he was sorry for what he had done, but
still, Melissa couldn't find a way to forgive the man she once
loved.

"So what happens now?" Melissa asked.

"You leave town tonight, because if you stay you already
know what's going to happen," he answered sharply.

"Pop, I was really hoping this could work," she said, looking
him in his eyes.

"It's too late for all that now," Pop said looking the woman
in her eyes. "If I could go back and do it all over again you
know I would. I would just start over from scratch and just

stayed broke, but then you probably wouldn't even be standing here with me," he chuckled.

"I love you, Pop, always have and I always will," Melissa said as she gave him a big bear hug.

In her heart she knew this was the last time she would ever hug Pop again in this lifetime, so she made sure it was a good one.

"You need me to drive you to the airport?" Pop asked with his head hung low.

"Nah, my car is right outside, I'll just take myself," she answered quickly.

"You need money to get on the plane?" he asked.

"Nah, I'm straight Pop, you just make sure you take care of yourself, and try not to ruin another good woman's life," Melissa said as she walked out of the hotel room into the pouring rain.

Pop stood in the doorway and just watched Melissa walk out into the rain and out of his life. His eyes began to water, but he had been through so much pain in his life that tears were far from falling from his eyes. He just wished that it didn't have to end like this.

Melissa stepped outside and couldn't believe what she just heard. How could the man she loved so much kill her sister? The way she found out just seemed to make it ten times worse.

I should go to the police and tell on all their asses, Melissa thought as hurt crept into her heart. She wanted to hate Pop but something inside of her wouldn't let her.

"I fuckin' hate him!" Melissa yelled out, trying to convince herself as she fished inside her purse for her keys. As soon as her key touched the lock, Melissa felt a gloved hand cover her mouth and something sharp poking her in her neck.

"Bitch, don't even think about screaming," Rusty warned

as he quickly escorted Melissa over to where his van was parked.

"I knew that nigga was gonna bitch up," Rusty said, laughing as he violently shoved Melissa in the back of the van.

"Bitch, lay on your stomach!" he demanded as he duct-taped both of her hands together, followed by her mouth.

"You can scream all you want now," Rusty chuckled as he began checking out Melissa's sexy, meaty thighs. By the look on his face she could already see what he was thinking. She tried to scream but nothing came out but a muffled noise.

"No one can hear you, sweetheart," Rusty said with a smile as he unbuttoned her jeans and removed them. He then reached down and ripped Melissa's thong off.

"Damn!" Rusty huffed when he saw how fat and pretty Melissa's pussy lips were.

"No wonder that nigga Pop tried to keep you all to himself," he said as he roughly separated Melissa's legs and began eating her pussy like he was a porn star. Melissa was trying to scream but with the tape on her mouth it made her screams sound more like moans, and that only excited Rusty even more. He continued to lick and suck on Melissa's clit as he inserted two fingers inside her pussy, and began to slide them in and out in a fast, rough motion.

Rusty then stood up, staring at her. He tasted his fingers as he unbuckled his belt with his other hand.

"You been fuckin' with that young nigga Pop, now it's time to show you how a real man puts it down," Rusty said, pulling out his dick.

"Yeah, you like that don't you?" He smiled as he stroked it. Rusty thought about putting on a condom but since he was going to kill her afterward anyway he decided against it.

"Open up those legs for daddy," Rusty said, sounding like

a pervert. Just as he slipped the head inside of her love tunnel he felt a blunt object connect with the back of his head. Once Rusty hit the ground Pop proceeded to pistol-whip the man until he was sure he was out cold. Pop then quickly snatched the tape off of Melissa's mouth, then cut the tape from off her wrist.

"Get your shit and get the fuck outta here," Pop said, feeling bad for the woman. It seemed like bad things only happened to good people.

Once Melissa was free she quickly ran over to Rusty's body and began to stomp him in his face, barefoot.

"What the fuck is you doing?" Pop asked, grabbing Melissa by her shoulders.

"Put your clothes back on and get the fuck out of here."

Once Pop let Melissa go she quickly turned and smacked the shit out of him.

"Fuck you, Pop, I wish never fuckin' met you," she said as her voice cracked as she began putting her clothes back on. Pop wanted to tell Melissa how sorry he was but he knew it wouldn't do him no good so instead he decided to just stay out of her way. Deep down inside he felt like shit. "All I wanted to do was just make a little money, get a few women, and leave town and start up a business," he said to himself, wondering how the hell things got so messed up so fast. Once Melissa had all her clothes on she stormed past Pop, never looking back.

"Leave this fucked-up city and never come back you hear me?" Pop yelled out. "Never come back . . ." His voice faded into a whisper as he watched her storm out the parking lot and out of his life forever.

"I love you, baby," Pop said in a volume that only he could hear. He looked over and saw Rusty still laid out on the ground. He knew he had just crossed the line but his heart was too good to let Melissa go out like that. Melissa was a good girl and the sad part was she wasn't even thinking about going to the police or at least back then she wasn't.

Forty-eight hours had passed and Tito had finally come up with the perfect plan on how he was going to kill Fresh. Tito doubled-parked his Acura in front of the projects. After sitting there for twenty minutes he saw the person he was looking for. Immediately he popped his trunk and slid out the driver door.

When Pooh saw Tito power-walking in his direction, he damn near shitted on himself. His first thought was to reach for the .380 he had tucked in his boot, but he knew by the time he got to his weapon he would already have three hot slugs in his back, so instead Pooh tried to act regular.

"Oh, shit, my nigga, Tito what's poppin'?" Pooh said, extending his hand to give the man some dap.

"Put ya fuckin' hand down you already know what's poppin'," Tito responded, placing his P89 to the big man's ribs.

"Come on, man, all this shit isn't called for," Pooh pleaded.

"Of course it is," Tito shot back as he screwed a silencer on his P89.

"I don't even fuck with Fresh no more I swear to God," Pooh said, pleading for his life.

"I know," Tito began calmly. "Just get in the trunk."

"Nah, B, you going to have to shoot me right here 'cause I'm not getting in that—"

Before Pooh knew it his thigh had a hole in it. Tito quickly shoved the big man in the trunk before he could drop to the ground.

As Tito tossed Pooh in the trunk, he noticed the .380 hanging out of the man's boot. Quickly Tito unarmed the big man and slammed the trunk shut.

"Fat mu'fucka," Tito snarled as he jumped in the driver's seat of his Acura and peeled off.

"Wherever I catch that nigga that's where I'm leaving him," Rusty huffed, still mad that Pop had fucked him up. But he was really mad that Pop had interrupted right before he was about to get some of Melissa's sweet pussy.

"Wow that's crazy," Fresh said, leaning back in his chair before he continued. "I hate to do this but Pop is leaving me no choice, put the word out there fifteen stacks for whoever takes Pop's life," he said, looking at Rusty's scarred-up face.

Deep down inside Fresh wished that it was something that he could do to help Pop, "cause he really liked the young man, but he knew if he didn't handle this situation properly the streets would take it as a sign of weakness.

"Fuck it, Pop just going to have to bite the bullet on this one," Fresh said to himself as he began to prepare a backup plan. Just in case anything went wrong he would have another option to address the situation.

Melissa pulled up in front of the police station and let the engine die. Her eyes were bloodshot red from all the crying she had been doing. She still couldn't believe Pop killed her sister, but yet she was still thankful that he saved her life the other night. She still had no answers to her questions, like why would Fresh want Amanda murdered. She and Amanda talked to each other about everything and snitching was never a topic. But now Melissa had no choice but to do what she had to do. She loved Pop to death but in her book family came first and even though Amanda was dead she was still family. Before Melissa exited her vehicle she pulled out her cell phone and dialed Pop's number. It rung a few times then went straight to his voice mail so she decided to leave a message.

"Hey, Pop, it's me Melissa. I just wanted to say thank you for what you did for me last night." She paused. "They say everything that happens, it happens for a reason, but as I sit here in front of this police station I can't seem to come up with a reason not to go inside and spill my guts. This message is just to let you know that I love you dearly and you will always have my heart, but on the other hand, I have to do what I have to do and as of right now the police are the only ones who can help me . . . by the time you hear this message I'll be done telling the police everything that I know. So what I need you to do is take the advice that you gave me the other night—Leave this fucked-up city and never come back!" Melissa sobbed as she ended the call.

"A yo, give me five of those mountain bikes right there," Pop said to the salesman.

"Which ones?"

"It don't matter just give me five of them mu'fuckas," Pop snarled, tossing the money on the counter.

For the past three days Pop had not been in the best of moods. He no longer had any positive thoughts left in his brain, only negative ones, not to mention he was about to go crazy from being paranoid. Every five seconds he found himself looking over his shoulders.

"Yo, y'all come get these bikes," Pop said, signaling for the five kids to come inside the store. "Yo, hook these kids up," Pop said to the salesman as he exited the store.

As soon as Pop stepped outside the store something just didn't feel right. He quickly hopped in his Benz. "I think I'm going to lay low for these last few days," he said to himself as stepped on the gas, heading home. As Pop drove home he picked up his phone and saw that he had a missed call from Melissa along with a message. He quickly listened to the message. After he heard the message that she had left him all he could do was chuckle.

"Fuck it," Pop said out loud. *What else could go wrong?* he thought as he weaved in and out of lanes. After listening to that message Pop knew he had to leave town and do it fast. Jail wasn't in his plans nor was getting killed, so his brain was racing a thousand miles per second. He didn't know what his next move was, but he knew he had to make a move and make it fast.

Pop pulled into the hotel parking lot that he and Nika had been staying in and let the engine die. He looked over both shoulders before he entered his room. Not only did he have Fresh and the goons out looking for him, but now he also had to worry about the cops looking to pick him up.

At the end of the day Pop wasn't even really mad at Melissa for going to the police. Once certain lines are crossed there ain't no telling what a person will do or is willing to do. He just knew that from now on he had to stay on point.

When Pooh woke up he found himself in some kind of basement, tied to a chair. "What the fuck is going on?" Pooh yelled, waiting for an answer.

Immediately Pooh defecated on himself when he felt the

Taser come in contact with his stomach. Pooh's body jerked and shook uncontrollably until Tito removed the Taser from his stomach.

"You ready to talk now?" Tito asked.

"I already told you I don't know where to find Fresh," Pooh whined as tears rolled down his cheek. After ten minutes of hitting Pooh with the Taser it was time for something a little more powerful.

"I don't know why you want to do things the hard way," Tito chuckled as he removed a nail gun from his duffel bag.

"Come on, Tito, we were like brothers back in the day," Pooh cried.

"This ain't back in the day no more," Tito said coldly as he sent a nail through Pooh's shoulder. Pooh screamed at the top of his lungs as he felt pain shoot through his whole body.

"Okay, okay, I'll tell you whatever you want to know," Pooh squealed as a long line of slob hung from his chin.

"All I want to know is when can I find Fresh when he's alone?"

"The only time he's alone is when he goes to see Vanessa," Pooh said as he broking into a coughing fit.

"Who the fuck is Vanessa?" Tito asked.

"Some chick Fresh be messing with from the Bronx. She live out in Queensbridge."

"Now how hard was that?" Tito asked as he untied Pooh's right hand and the man wrote down the address as Tito held a pen and pad up close to him.

"There's the address now untie me," Pooh demanded.

"I'm sorry but I can't do that," Tito said as he placed the nail gun to Pooh's head, and pulled the trigger several times.

Tito didn't even stay to see Pooh's body hit the floor, once he pulled the trigger he was on his way to avenge his mother's death.

***

All day Tito sat parked at the address that Pooh had given him. "What the fuck is taking this mu'fucka so long?" he said out loud, looking at his windshield wipers wipe away the raindrops.

Fifteen minutes later, Tito noticed a black Navigator stop directly in front of the address Pooh had given him. Tito's hands immediately started sweating as he tightened his grip on his shotgun, hoping this was his target pulling up.

Rusty stepped out of the driver's side of the navigator holding a .45 at his side. He quickly walked around to the other side to open up the back door for Fresh, but before he did he scanned the block thoroughly. "Ain't nobody out here on a rainy day like this," he said to himself as he opened the back door. Once Tito laid eyes on Fresh he made his move. He slid out of his vehicle, and began a slow jog so he could get closer to his target for a possible better shot.

The sound of someone's foot splashing in a puddle quickly told Rusty that he and Fresh weren't the only ones outside.

"Watch your back, Fresh!" Rusty yelled as he turned around, raising his .45. Unfortunately, for him he didn't turn around quick enough. Tito pulled the trigger on his shotgun, lighting up the street with a loud, roaring noise.

Fresh just watched as the power from the shotgun lifted Rusty off his feet and hurled him backward. Rusty's body hit the ground like a rag doll and skidded until it crashed the curb. Instantly Fresh pulled out his .380 and sent two shots in Tito's direction as he dodged a fireball from Tito's shotgun.

Fresh's heart was beating a thousand miles per second as he took cover behind a parked car. A shiver of fear ran down his spine as he heard the shotgun blast blow out the windows of the parked car he stood behind as glass rained on top of his head.

"Stop hiding, you fuckin' pussy!" Tito yelled as he slowly moved closer to the parked car with caution.

Vanessa had just got out of the shower when she heard the first thunderous gunshot go off. Once she heard the shots she knew Fresh had something to do with it.

"Lord, please don't let my baby be hurt," Vanessa prayed out loud as she ran to the window in her towel to see what was going on. Her heart dropped instantly when she saw the unknown gunman closing in on Fresh. Without hesitation Vanessa ran to her closet and grabbed the 9 mm that Fresh had given her for emergencies only, and headed back toward the window.

The rain was coming down so hard Tito knew in order to get a good shot he was going to have to get closer to Fresh, he was even willing to take a shot to give one. Before Tito could take another step he heard multiple gunshots go off as they came raining down in his chest, sending him crashing to the ground.

As Tito laid on the wet ground he heard a woman's voice from up above scream, "I love you, Fresh." He couldn't make out the face of the person who shot him; all he could see was a blurry picture of the shooter in the window. With his last bit of strength Tito aimed his shotgun at the blurry picture and pulled the trigger.

The shot blew half of Vanessa's face off as she fell out of the second-floor window, landing right next to Fresh. The sight of Vanessa's mutilated face caused Fresh to throw up the Popeyes fried chicken he consumed earlier.

"Damn, boo," Fresh sneered as he looked at his shorty laying on the wet ground, stretched out.

"Fuck!" Fresh screamed out as he heard the sound of police sirens getting louder and louder.

He quickly made his way to Tito and stood over his body.

"A real leader takes care of his peoples," Tito slurred, letting out a weak cough, follow by a wicked smirk.

Fresh didn't respond, instead he emptied his clip in Tito's face.

"Bitch-ass nigga," Fresh growled as he ran and hopped in the driver's seat of the Navigator. Before he could even get a block away a police car crashed into him from the side causing the back of his SUV to swerve in the wrong direction. Fresh tried to ignore the crash but a second cop car stopped directly in front of him, blocking his path.

"Aww shit," Fresh cursed as he reached for his .380 until he remembered that it was empty. Left with no choice, he surrendered as he placed his hands on the steering wheel.

Chapter Twenty

The Big Day

"Yo, you got everything?" Pop asked as he placed the $200,000 dollars he had saved up in a duffel bag.

"Yeah, I got everything," Nika replied with a smile on her face. This was the happiest day of Nika's life—she was leaving New York with the man she loved, and had no plans on returning.

Pop placed his 9 mm in his waistband for backup, but his main weapon of choice was an AK-47. Way too much shit had been jumping off for Pop to take a chance, all he wanted to do was leave town in one piece.

"Baby, pull the car up in front of my mother's building, I'm going to run over there and leave her a couple of dollars," Pop said as he handed Nika his AK-47.

When Pop stepped outside he glanced at his watch that read 7:05 A.M. Pop was trying to leave town early to avoid any problems. As he approached his mother's building he noticed little Brittany sitting outside on the bench.

"What the fuck is she doing out here so early?" Pop wondered as he approached his little sister.

"What you doing out here so early?" he asked curiously.

"I'm just getting some fresh air," little Brittany answered with her head down.

"At seven o'clock in the morning?" Pop asked as he studied the little girl. As he looked his little sister up and down he noticed that she was sporting a fresh black-and-blue bruise on her neck.

"Who been hitting you like this?" Pop asked.

"Mommy's new boyfriend," little Brittany whispered, looking at the ground.

"What else has that fool been doing to you?" Pop asked curiously. The look on little Brittany's face answered Pop's question.

"He upstairs right now?" he asked. Little Brittany didn't speak, she just nodded yes.

"Wait right here I'll be right back," Pop stated as he headed upstairs. Once he reached his mother's floor he quickly snatched his 9 mm from his waistband as he unlocked the front door with his key.

The smell of urine mixed with dirty clothes quickly assaulted Pop's nose. He made his way down the dark hallway until he reached his mother's room. Teresa and her boyfriend both jumped when they saw the bedroom door fly open.

"Mu'fucka, you don't know how to knock?" the boyfriend barked, whipping the crust from his eyes. Instantly Pop exploded at the sound of the man's voice.

"What?" Pop asked, moving in closer.

"Nigga, is you deaf mu'fucka? I said—"

A bullet to the man's head quickly took the life out of his body. "You should be ashamed of yourself—how you let this pervert touch Brittany?" Pop asked, aiming his smoking pistol at his mother.

"That little bitch is lying, what did she tell you?" Teresa asked, defensively frowning her face up at her son. "I hope it was worth it, fool, 'cause now you going to spend the rest of your miserable life behind bars. I already told you I didn't want you in my house again," Teresa snapped as she picked up the phone.

"None of us asked to be here," Pop said flatly as a tear escaped his eye.

"Yeah, and I didn't ask you to be in my house right now, and don't flatter yourself because if I had the money for an abortion trust me you wouldn't be standing here right now," Teresa added as she dialed 911.

"I really think you should of had the abortion," Pop said as he pulled trigger until there were no bullets left in the 9 mm.

"Fuckin' lowlife scumbag," Pop said under his breath as he took a look at the apartment he grew up in for the last time before making his exit.

When Pop made it back downstairs he quickly made his way over toward his sister and grabbed her by the wrist. "Come on, you coming with me," Pop said as he grabbed little Brittany's hand and led her to the Benz that awaited them.

"Yo, it's been a change of plans," Pop said as he slid in the passenger side of the Benz. "Brittany is coming with us."

By the look on Pop's face, Nika could tell that he just did something crazy. "Yo, take me to the block so I can see my nigga Jason real quick," Pop ordered as he reloaded his 9 mm.

After about fifteen minutes of driving Nika noticed two Dodge Chargers seemed to be following her.

"Baby, I think we got some company," Nika said, looking through the rearview mirror.

"What you see, baby?" Pop asked, trying to look through the small side mirror so it didn't look obvious.

"Two Chargers riding side by side, they been in the rearview mirror for the last fifteen minutes," Nika answered.

"Find out if they following us or not," Pop said calmly as he grabbed the AK-47 from off the floor and placed it on his lap.

"No problem, baby," Nika responded as she quickly swerved two lanes over, putting the pedal to the metal. Without hesitation the two Dodge Chargers did whatever the Benz did as if they were playing a game of follow the leader.

"Yeah, they definitely following us, baby," Nika replied, still looking through the rearview mirror.

"A'ight, get off the next exit," Pop ordered as he said a quick prayer.

"A yo, pull over right there in front of the train station," he said, pointing to the train station.

"A'ight, this is what we going to do, I want you to take Brittany, and get on the train," he told her.

"What? You must be crazy," Nika shot back. "I'm not leaving you, we in this shit together."

"Listen, we ain't going to make it driving. I want you and Brittany to take the train to forty-deuce (Forty-second Street) and grab us three Greyhound tickets going to Miami. It's eight o'clock now, get the tickets for nine o'clock and I'll meet you at the station before the bus leaves the station, a'ight?" Pop said.

"Pop, I don't want to leave you," Nika cried out as the tears came rolling down her face.

"You have to, baby, I don't give a fuck what happens at nine o'clock, you better be on that bus," Pop said as he handed Nika the duffel bag full of money.

"You better be there before that fuckin' bus takes off, Pop," she warned.

"Listen, baby, I'm going to do whatever it takes to catch that bus," Pop assured Nika as he placed a big, wet juicy kiss on her lips.

"I love you, Pop," Nika said as she slid out the driver's door, grabbed Brittany, and headed down the subway steps.

Once Nika disappeared out of Pop's eyesight, he quickly slid over to the driver's seat. He looked through his rearview mirror as he saw the two Chargers sitting idly a block away.

"Let's go, mu'fuckas, it's showtime," he said out loud as he pulled out into traffic.

After about twenty minutes of testing the driving skills of the hitmen, Pop finally pulled up on his block.

As soon as Jason saw the Benz pull up he quickly grabbed the book bag that sat next to him, and made his way over to the driver's side window.

"Pop, what's good my nigga?" Jason asked as he tossed the book bag on the floor of the Benz. "That's sixty Gs right there. A little going-away present for you," Jason joked.

"Yo, you see them two Chargers back there?" Pop asked, looking through his rearview mirror.

"Yeah, I see them," Jason answered.

"Them mu'fuckas been following me for the past thirty minutes," Pop informed.

"So how you want to handle this?" Jason asked, down for whatever.

"I'm not sure yet but I'm going to have to do something quick 'cause my bus is leaving for Miami in thirty minutes," Pop explained.

"Yo, put your head down, here these mu'fuckas come," Jason yelled as he pulled out his cannon.

Once both of the Chargers got close enough to the Benz, the back windows rolled down, and out came a masked man holding a Mac 10 in each hand. Jason tried to hold his boss down but he was no match for the two masked man. The bullets from the Mac 10's ripped through Jason's body effortlessly.

Pop quickly took cover as the Mac 10 bullets riddled and rocked the Benz back and forth.

Pop clutched his AK as broken glass showered over him.

Once the gunfire paused, Pop slid out his Benz but still remained low as he peeked around the car so he could see what was going on. When Pop took his peek all he saw was opportunity. Without hesitation he sprung up from behind the Benz, blasting the AK. The machine gun filled the streets with a deadly roar. The bullets from the AK destroyed any and everything in its path, including innocent bystanders.

Once Pop ran out of bullets, he quickly hopped back in his bullet-filled Benz and peeled off. As he tried to make his getaway he noticed in his rearview mirror two cops cars tailing him. Pop didn't give a fuck; he was going to catch his bus by any means necessary. He quickly made a sharp left turn down a one way street. To his surprise, the two cop cars followed him down a oneway street at top speed.

"Let's do this, mu'fuckas," Pop said out loud as he swerved out of the way of a oncoming vehicle as he turned into oncoming traffic.

Out of reflex Pop swerved away from a head-on collision with a van by a fingernail. "Oh, shit," Pop yelled as he headed full speed toward a busy intersection. As he reached the intersection, he closed his eyes and prayed he would make it across safely.

Seconds later Pop found out that his prayers wouldn't be answered, as his neck jerked violently from side to side from the series of hits that his car took. "Aww shit," he slurred as he felt warm blood running down his face.

Pop tried to use his right hand to pick the book bag up from off the floor, but his dislocated shoulder disagreed with the decision. With time working against him Pop grabbed the book bag with his left hand and placed it over his shoulder. He tried to get out of the vehicle but the driver's side door was jammed shut from the accident. Without thinking twice

Pop slid out the window until his body slammed against the concrete.

Pop quickly picked himself up off the ground and began jogging down the street. "Fuck that, I ain't going to jail," he kept telling himself as he continued jogging down the street.

"Somebody stop that man!" a witness screamed out, pointing at the man with blood covering his face running down the street. Pop looked at his watch that read 8:53 A.M. "Don't worry, baby, I'm coming," he screamed out as if Nika could really hear him. He knew the bus station was only a couple of blocks away, his chances of making it were about sixty-forty.

"Miss, may I have you and your daughter's ticket?" the fat bus driver asked.

"I'm sorry sir, here you go," Nika responded, handing the bus driver three tickets.

"My boyfriend is running a little late. Here's his ticket, can you give him like ten more minutes before you pull off, please?" Nika asked in a begging tone.

"Ten minutes and that's all," the bus driver said firmly.

"Okay, thank you so much," Nika said, feeling a little better inside.

"Freeze, don't move!" a cop yelled, looking at the bloody man running down the street.

Pop ignored the officer and quickly sent two reckless shots in the cop's direction as he made a detour and cut through the park. As Pop cut through the park he noticed all the kids looking at him. The thought of those kids going through what he went through as a kid brought tears to his eyes. If he had a head start as a kid he probably wouldn't be getting chased at this very moment.

Pop looked over his shoulder and saw four officers running full speed in his direction. He had to do something and do it quick. He quickly ran toward the kids and unzipped his book bag. With no regrets he tossed the bag into the air and watched as money flew in every direction. Immediately all the kids, and their parents scrambled for their share of the money.

With that being done Pop managed to escape from out of the park. Once back on the streets, he did the best he could to clean his face with his shirt as he continued en route to the bus station. Pop no longer jogged, but instead he walked at a fast pace so he could try to blend in with other pedestrians.

"Excuse me, bus driver, can you please wait for five more minutes?" Nika begged the fat bus driver.

"I'm sorry, miss, but I have to get this bus on the road, I've waited for as long as I could," the bus driver replied as he pulled out of the bus terminal.

Not knowing what else to do Nika went back to her seat and pulled out her cell phone. "Pop, you better answer," she said to herself as she heard it ringing on the other line.

A smile appeared across Pop's face as he stood a block away from the bus terminal. That smile quickly disappeared when he felt his Nextel vibrating. He looked at the phone and saw Nika's name flashing across the screen.

"Baby, I'm here," he said, out of breath.

"Where are you? I don't see you," Nika yelled into the receiver.

"I'm right outside the bus terminal," he answered.

"Stay right there we coming out the terminal now I'm going to tell the bus driver to stop the bus," Nika said excitedly. Before Pop could say another word a hard blow hit him in the back, causing him to drop to his knees. Instantly Pop's vision got blurry as he saw a Greyhound bus cruise out of the bus terminal. "Stop the fuckin' bus!" Nika yelled as she ran toward the front of the bus.

Once the door opened Nika kicked off her four-inch heels and ran toward her man who stood on his knees in the middle of the street.

A huge smile came across Pop's face as he saw his woman running to his rescue. "Damn, I love that girl," was Pop's last thought. Seconds later three shots to Pop's body sent his face crashing into the pavement.

"I finally got that fool," the Chinese detective said as he slid his smoking .357 back in his holster, looking like Robo cop, then acting like nothing never even happened.

"*Noooo!*" Nika screamed at the top of her lungs.

"Y'all didn't have to shoot him, he already surrendered," Nika screamed out as she cradled Pop's head in her arms. Seconds later little Brittany came walking up, carrying the duffel bag full of money.

She didn't say anything; she just looked down at her favorite brother laying in a pool of his own blood. "Nika, he did this so we wouldn't have to struggle no more," little Brittany said, wiping the tears from her eyes.

"I know sweetie," Nika responded as endless tears rolled down her cheeks. "But they didn't have to kill him he was already on his knee,s goddamn!" she whispered.

"Just know he's in a better place now," little Brittany said, looking up at the sky.

"Hello, miss, I'm going to need to ask you a few questions," the Chinese detective said, placing a hand on Nika's shoulder.

"Get your fuckin' hands off me," Nika growled as she hog spit in the detective's face.

"Come on, little Brittany, let's get out of here," Nika said as she grabbed the little girl's hand, leading her to the corner where they disappeared in the backseat of a cab, never to be seen again in New York City.

Chapter Twenty-one

4 Years Later

Nika sat watching all the kids enjoy themselves in the after-school center that she had been running for the past three years. It was truly a blessing to see all the kids playing nicely with one another and never wanting to go home.

She knew if Pop was still alive he would have loved it in Miami because she loved every minute of it. She just wished Pop was around to share it with her. In memory of Pop, when you stepped inside the after-school center there was a huge picture of him posted on the wall. Every time Nika looked at that picture she felt as if he was watching her from up above. Even though Pop was gone Nika made sure she kept his dream alive. If he was still alive she knew he would have been proud of her.

"I love you, baby, none of this would be possible if it wasn't for you," Nika whispered as she blew Pop a kiss.

After everything went down, Melissa moved to North Carolina where she became a registered nurse. She left the city of New York hoping to start her life over again with no thoughts of ever returning. She still thought about Pop and her sister every now and then, but most of the time she would pile herself with work so she didn't have to think about her past.

***

Two years into his bid Fresh got stabbed to death in the shower in an upstate correctional facility by one of Tito's old cell mates. Karma is real.

Bamboo reigned supreme in the end and continued to make money in the city . . . still living the fast life. His wife always begged him to leave the game, but the allure is too strong and the only thing that will take him out is death or prison.

SOMETHING TO THINK ABOUT

Everybody wants to come-up in life. It all depends on how you go about coming up, and what you're willing and not willing to do in order to come-up.

The ball is in your court, either you gonna ball hard or fall hard.

Just ask yourself this one question.

How far are you willing to go in order to come-up?

Notes